DOCTOR WHO
AND THE CRUSADERS

THE CHANGING FACE OF DOCTOR WHO

The cover illustration and others contained within
this book portray the first DOCTOR WHO whose physical
appearance was later transformed when he discarded
his worn-out body in favour of a new one.

A TARGET ADVENTURE

DOCTOR WHO AND THE CRUSADERS

Based on the BBC television serial by
David Whitaker by arrangement with the BBC

DAVID WHITAKER

Illustrated by Henry Fox

a division of
Universal-Tandem Publishing Co., Ltd.
14 Gloucester Road, London SW7 4RD

First published in Great Britain by Frederick Muller, Ltd., 1965

First published in this edition by
Universal-Tandem Publishing Co., Ltd., 1973

ISBN 0 426 10137 5

Printed in Great Britain by The Anchor Press, Ltd.,
and bound by Wm. Brendon & Son, Ltd.,
both of Tiptree, Essex

Prologue

As swiftly and as silently as a shadow, Doctor Who's Space and Time ship, *Tardis*, appeared on a succession of planets each as different as the pebbles on a beach, stayed awhile and then vanished, as mysteriously as it had come. And whatever alien world it was that received him and his fellow travellers, and however well or badly they were treated, the Doctor always set things to rights, put down injustice, encouraged dignity, fair treatment and respect.

But there had been changes inside the ship. Susan had gone, left behind in an England all but destroyed in the twenty-first century when the Daleks had attempted the conquest of Earth, an invasion only just foiled by the Doctor. No decision was more difficult for Susan or easier for her grandfather, who knew in his heart that she must share her future with David Cameron, a young man she had met and fallen in love with during that terrible struggle between the Doctor and his arch-enemies.

Only Ian and Barbara, kidnapped by the Doctor from their lives in the England of the 1960s and now his close friends, knew the real aching sadness the loss of Susan meant to the old man, and it was they who persuaded him to take on as a passenger a young girl named Vicki whom they rescued from the planet Dido. And, as the Doctor grew more interested in the little, fair-haired orphan and devoted himself to her care and well-being (which Vicki repaid with a totally single-minded love and respect) his friends were secretly overjoyed to see a new and vigorous spring in the Doctor's step, a happy gleam in his eye and a fresh interest in the unknown adventures that lay ahead.

Ian and Barbara had changed too. Ian was now a deeply tanned bronze, his body trained to the last minute, no single trace remaining of the ordinary Londoner he had once been. But the alteration wasn't confined to muscle and sinew alone. Ian had encountered situations beyond the concept of any young man of his age. He had faced dangers and been forced to make decisions a countless number of times, where not only his own life, but the lives of others, stood in peril. Experience had proved to him that strength and fitness alone weren't enough in the sort of emergencies he had to handle, and so he had turned his new life to advantage, learned from it and improved by it, until his brain was sharp and active, tuned to deal with whatever problems might present themselves.

The change in Barbara was entirely different; harder, perhaps, to find; a much more subtle thing. For unlike Ian, she could have been put back in London in the old life she had known, among friends and acquaintances and not one of them would have found any major alterations to puzzle or bewilder them. The golden tan on her skin might have come from a long holiday in the West Indies. Her superb physical condition could be explained away by regular visits to a gymnasium. For what was totally new in Barbara grew and fostered inside the girl. She had always had that sense of mystery about her, even on Earth in her own time; she had always been very beautiful, her mind had always reached ahead for answers and conclusions while others struggled to grasp the situation. Now, life inside the *Tardis* had given full reign to her air of mystery, and the adventures outside it had deepened her love for life in all its various forms, maturing her sense of values, giving her the ability to taste the joys and sorrows of existence to the absolute last drop. Where her face and form had conjured up beauty in the eye of any beholder, now beauty radiated from within and trebled her physical attractions, making her the admiration and desire of all who met her. But always her eyes turned to Ian and their hands were ready to reach out and touch, for, whatever world of the future enmeshed them, they knew their destinies were bound up in each other – the one sure thing, fixed and unalterable, in the ever-changing life with the Doctor.

The question of change itself became the subject of a conversation one evening in the *Tardis*, between Ian and the Doctor. Barbara and Vicki were playing a game of Martian chess – a complicated affair with seventy-two pieces – while the two men rested on a Victorian chaise-longue facing the centre-control column of the ship, for the Doctor's eyes were never far away from his precious dials and instruments. Behind them lay the adventure of the talking stones of the tiny planet of Tyron, in the seventeenth galaxy. Around them, the ship shivered faintly as it hurled itself through Space and Time. A dozen minute tape-recorder spools whirled frantically on one side, while hundreds of little bulbs on the central control column glowed intermittently, in a never-ending sequence. The stately Ormulu clock ticked its needless way through a time pattern which had no meaning, kept in the ship purely for decoration. On the other side of it, some twenty feet away on a tall marble column, stood the magnificent bust of Napoleon Bonaparte. The pale gold of the interior lighting of the *Tardis* shone down on the travellers like warm afternoon sunshine.

The Doctor shifted his feet impatiently and then leaned towards the Martian chess-board, darting out a rigid finger.

'You're forgetting the one important rule, Vicki, my dear,' he said testily. 'To marry your Princess to an opposing Lord, you must bring up your Priest.' He smiled apologetically at Barbara, as Vicki nodded excitedly, moved up one of her pieces and captured an enemy Lord.

'I'm sorry, Barbara, but you did leave yourself open.'
Barbara looked at him indignantly.

'I was planning to marry my Captain to her Duchess. Now you've made me lose a dowry.'

The two girls started to bargain over the forfeit as the Doctor sat back.

'I'd better keep myself to myself,' he muttered to Ian. He wriggled himself into a more comfortable position, crossing one leg over the other and folding his arms. The polish on his elastic-sided boots gleamed beneath the immaculate spats. The perfectly tied cravat sat comfortably beneath the stiff, white wing-collar, enhanced by a pearl stick-pin. No speck of dust or tiny crease were anywhere in evidence on his tapered black jacket, with its edges bound in black silk, or on the narrow trousers, patterned in black-and-white check. The long, silver hair hung down from the proudly held head, obscuring the back of his coat collar. Gold pince-nez, attached around the neck by a thin, black satin tape, completed the picture Ian and Barbara had always known. For the Doctor's favourite costume was that of the Edwardian, English gentleman of the early nineteen hundreds. Ian had always thought the Doctor might have stepped straight out of the drawings of the famous magazines of the period, *The Strand* or *Vanity Fair*. And as Ian marvelled (for about the thousandth time!) at the Doctor's obsession with that one, short period of life on Earth, when he had all space from which to choose, it brought a question to his lips he had often wished to have answered.

'It's often puzzled me how it is, Doctor, that we can visit all these different worlds and *affect* the course of life. You must confess we have interfered, often in quite a major kind of way.'

'Always for the best intentions, and generally we've succeeded,' murmured the old man. Ian nodded.

'That really isn't my point, though. Why is it that when we land on earth, with all the pre-knowledge of history at our disposal, we can't right one single wrong, make good the bad or change one tiny evil? Why are we able to do these things on other planets and not on Earth?'

Barbara and Vicki forgot their game and stared at the Doctor, who pressed the fingers of his hands together and thought for a moment before replying.

'You see, Chesterton,' he said eventually, 'the fascination your planet has for me is that its Time pattern, that is, past, present and future, is all one – like a long, winding mountain path. When the four of us land at any given point on that path, we are still only climbers. Time is our guide. As climbers we may observe the scenery. We may know a little of what is around a coming corner. But we cannot stop the landslides, for we are roped completely to Time and must be led by it. All we can do is observe.'

'What would happen if we cut those ropes and tried to change something?' asked Vicki.

'Warn Napoleon he would lose at Waterloo?' smiled the Doctor. 'It wouldn't have any effect. Bonaparte would still believe he could win and ignore the warning.'

'Suppose one were to assassinate Adolf Hitler in 1930, then?' suggested Barbara. The Doctor shook his head.

'But Hitler wasn't assassinated in 1930, was he? No, Barbara, it would be impossible. Once we are on Earth, we become a part of the history that is being created and we are as subject to its laws as the people who are living in that period.'

'Then we can never die on Earth,' said Ian.

The Doctor said, 'We do not have everlasting lives, my friend. Of course we can die on Earth or anywhere else, just as we can catch colds or suffer burns. Try and understand.'

The Doctor leaned forward and, as he did so, a part of his face slipped into a shadow.

'Often our escape clause on Earth has been that we have pre-knowledge that some awful catastrophe is going to happen. We would know when to leave Pompeii. We would not go fishing on the Somme river in the summer of 1916. We would not disguise ourselves as Phoenicians and live in Carthage in A.D. 648 and let ourselves be destroyed with the city by the Arabs. Or go for a sea-voyage in the *Titanic*.'

'Then we can do nothing for suffering,' murmured Barbara sadly. 'We can never help anyone on Earth or avert horrible wars.'

She looked up at the Doctor and was surprised to see a slight smile on his lips.

'There is a story about Clive of India,' the old man remarked casually, 'which tells how he attempted to commit suicide as a young man by putting a pistol to his head. Three times he pulled the trigger and each time the gun failed to explode. Yet whenever he turned it away, the pistol fired perfectly. As you know, Robert Clive did eventually take his own life in 1774. The point is that Time, that great regulator, refused to let the man die before things were done that had to be done.'

The Doctor held up a hand as all three of his friends started to speak.

'I know exactly what you're all about to say. Why do men like Lincoln and Kennedy, those two outstanding American Presidents, have their lives cut off short when everything lay before them, and they had shown themselves capable of doing good for their fellow men? How can I, or any person, answer that? It is too easy to say that the sharp, shocking manner of their deaths underlined heavily the contributions they made. Life, death, the pattern of Time, are eternal mysteries to us. Here you find one man squandering his talents on wholesale slaughter, evil and terrible acts of indignity. There, another makes every effort for peace, goodwill and happiness. Inventors of medicines and advantages for others are laughed into insane asylums. Discoverers of murder weapons die in old age as millionaires. True love is set aside, hatred seems to flower.'

'But that's appalling!' said Ian vehemently. 'That's the gloomiest view I've ever heard in my life.'

'My friend,' said the Doctor softly, 'it is only one small part of what I am saying. Time is constant. Look at history. You'll find the brave have their share of successes. You'll see that honesty, unselfishness and good works overflow in every generation. All I am saying is that what is going to happen on Earth *must* happen. If Rasputin is to die, no will to survive by that extraordinary man, no black arts, no personal power, can save him. Remember that they drugged Rasputin, shot him and then drowned him. No, don't try to understand why a fine man is cut off in his prime and an evil one prospers. Try to understand what benefit there is in observing history as it actually happens.'

'I don't see that there's any benefit in it at all,' muttered Ian, 'except for the fascination.' His eyes turned to the Doctor's. 'And, frankly,' he went on, with a more definite note in his voice, 'that isn't enough. We ought to be . . . to be doing things. Not just watching them happen.'

The Doctor stood up and walked over to the central control column. He stared down at the dials and switches for a few seconds and then turned to face them.

'We *are* doing something. We are learning. Why do people kill each other, steal from each other; rob, slander, hurt and destroy? Why do thousands upon thousands of young men hurl themselves at one another on a field of battle, each side sure in the justness of its cause? Until we know, until we can control greed, destructive ambition, hatred and the dozen and one other flaws that plague us, we are not worthy to breathe.'

The Doctor looked up at the ceiling of the Ship, his eyes strangely alight.

'The next time we visit Earth,' he said, 'I hope we encounter a situation where two men are opposed to each other, each for the best reasons.'

He suddenly looked down, turning his eyes from one to the other, with a directness that riveted their attentions.

'That is the only way to understand the folly, the stupidity and the horror of war. When both sides, in their own way, are totally right.'

He turned back to his controls, adjusting some, switching off others, until the *Tardis* began to shiver quite noticeably, responding now to a hundred thousand impulses of power, and a dozen different orders. The little Time and Space machine began to wheel in its path through the limitless pattern of the cosmos, describing a huge arc. Suns, satellites, stars and planets appeared and faded, all ignored, as the ship headed towards its objective – Earth!

CHAPTER ONE

Death in the Forest

The hawk turned in the sky above the forest, almost as if it were standing on its wing for a split second, and then darted down on its prey, its bold eyes of orange yellow glinting darkly in the bright sunlight; talons rigid and ready to catch and hold, the beak sharply poised to put down any struggle. It flashed lower, swooping to the right slightly, a compact weapon of destruction; slate grey above, a white touch on the nape, darkly streaked on its wings and tail. Beneath, the russet colour was broken by strips of brown. Whether the little bird, its prey, took fright because it recognized the danger of the colouring, whether it saw death in the broad, rounded wings and long, barred tail, or whether it simply sensed, as victims often do, a fast approaching end to its life, is something far beyond the knowledge of human beings. Sufficient to say, the little bird took fright and tried to elude its pursuer, with an urgent thrust of its tiny wing-span.

The man, whose red-gold hair was barely visible beneath his hunting cap, shaded his eyes and followed the battle eagerly. He watched as the birds circled, darted, joined and fell apart, noting a feather shoot away from the smaller of the two fighters and drift to the ground listlessly. Then the prey took flight and darted down into the trees, closely followed by the hawk, and both hunter and hunted disappeared. The man let his hand fall to his side and glanced at a companion dressed similarly in simple hunting clothes, who was sitting on the mossy ground of the forest glade, struggling to bend the clasp of a jewelled belt with his fingers. Another man, also in hunting clothes, leaned against a tree with his eyes closed, his face turned up into the sun, enjoying the peace of the afternoon, and he also received the amused attention of the one who had followed the battle in the skies with such fascination.

'It seems my friends have no interest in the battles of nature,' he murmured. His two friends looked at him, the one leaning against the tree flushing rather guiltily at his inattention. Before either of the men could reply, however, the hawk reappeared in the sky. Although normally rather quiet, the bird was clearly excited now, uttering a sharp 'taket, taket, taket', as if protesting at some insulting treatment it had received from within the depths of the forest, where it had pursued its prey. Finally, the hawk dived down and settled quietly on the extended arm of its master, who extracted a small leather pouch from his belt and slipped it over the bird's head.

'I am the only day and night for you, hunter,' murmured King Richard the First of England, stroking the back of the hawk's body gently. 'But why no success today?' He continued, reprovingly, 'I bring you all this way from England to see you made foolish. I hope this is not an omen, bird.'

He handed the hawk to a waiting servant. The man leaning against the tree folded his arms and watched the servant walk away with the bird on his arm.

'I wish I were a hawk, Sire, and Saladin my prey.'

'Now there is a subject for our troubadours and actors,' laughed the King. 'Speak to the Chamberlain about it, I beg you, de Marun.'

'I will, My Lord. And I shall have the players call the entertainment, "The Defeat of Saladin, the Sparrow of the East!"'

The three men's laughter echoed through the wood and the man who had been trying to bend the clasp of the jewel-studded gold belt, Sir William de Tornebu, put his work aside and joined in the merriment, until they heard the sound of footsteps through the bushes. Branches were thrust aside and a tall, dark-haired man, a sword held firmly in his right hand, stepped into view. Richard held up a hand in mock surrender.

'No, des Preaux, I will not fight today!'

Sir William des Preaux lowered the sword with a slight smile.

'I think he means to slay us all,' murmured de Marun.

'Aye, and eat us for his dinner,' added de Tornebu, who had returned to work on the clasp again. Des Preaux glanced at the three men and rather surprised them by not replying to their jokes in a similar vein.

'I have heard sounds in these woods, Sire,' he said seriously, walking over to the King. 'You are too far from Jaffa and the Saracens too near.'

The King shrugged, stooped down and picked up a skin of water and a silver goblet from a little pile of refreshments laid out by the servant. He poured himself a long drink of clear water and drank deeply.

'Have you seen any Saracens?' asked de Tornebu, and des Preaux shook his head.

'No, but I sense them about us. This wood might have been designed for ambush. We have none of Nature's warning voices on our side.' He looked at the three men, one after another, significantly. 'There is not one bird in a tree.'

'Put up your sword,' murmured the King. 'My hawk has frightened away the birds. Come, come, des Preaux, you sound like an old woman surrounded by shadows.' He spread himself on the ground, rummaged among the provisions and found a bunch of grapes and began to eat them. Des Preaux looked at him anxiously.

'I have put Alun and Luke de L'Etable with the horses, Sire. All is ready for the return to Jaffa.'

King Richard's eyes moved from his contemplation of the bunch of grapes and stared into those of the man with the sword coldly, the lazy air of relaxation dropping away from his reclining body and changing to a stiff tension. Des Preaux shifted uncomfortably, conscious that he had presumed to make a decision before referring it. But he held the King's gaze because of his genuine concern, and his belief that danger was everywhere around the man he had sworn to serve.

Richard said: 'We will stay here.'

There was a moment's pause as the two men stared at each other, the one completely certain of his right to decide, the other afraid to give way. Finally, des Preaux reddened and dropped his eyes. Immediately a change came over the King and he smiled. Not because he had won a battle of wills or because he had achieved his own purpose. Richard, although impulsive, was not the man to feel any triumph in succeeding when he had no chance to lose. The reason men followed him, fought and died for him, was that his fairness and judgement of character were acute.

'Yes, we will all stay here,' he continued, 'until, William the Wary, you recover your composure. And, I hope, your sense of humour.'

As the King and his three friends gathered around the refreshments and ate and drank, a man with a vivid scar running down the right side of his face, parted some bushes about a hundred yards away and peered at them. He watched the four men intently for a moment, let the bushes close together again and sank down under cover, beckoning slightly with one hand, each finger of which was holding a jewelled ring. His dark eyes glittered and there was an air of suppressed excitement written all over his swarthy face. The Saracen soldier he had commanded crept up to him, and lay beside him patiently.

'One of these four men is the English King, Malec Ric,' the man with the scar whispered. 'We will come at them at close quarters. They are dressed too much alike for me to tell which is the King and which are servants or friends. But one will declare himself as they fight for their lives. He who takes command is the King and he must be taken alive.'

He looked at the soldier beside him, their faces close together.

'Alive, do you understand?' he muttered viciously. The soldier licked his lips and nodded.

'Then get my men placed well, and when I move tell them they are all to show themselves. Now go!'

The man with the scar pushed at the soldier roughly, watched him squirm back the way he had come then turned his attentions to the unsuspecting men in the little forest clearing.

In another part of the wood, the *Tardis* found itself a clear patch and materialized, its safety precaution selector deliberately choosing a place well screened by tall thick bushes. It was one of the features of the Doctor's ship that it always assessed the place it landed in in one millionth of a second before it materialized, and was thus able to avoid appearing in busy streets or under water, or any of the hundred and one hazards which might endanger the safety of the ship and its occupants. Had its safety device been of a much wider sort, of course, it is more than likely it would have detected the presence of the coming struggle in the little forest outside Jaffa. But, of course, if its sensitivity had been so fine there would be no chronicles about Doctor Who.

Ian was first out of the ship. He crept over to the screen of tall bushes and peered through them. Barbara came across from the *Tardis* and stood beside him quietly.

'It's all right,' he said, 'I don't know where we are, but it looks like an ordinary wood.'

'The Doctor says we've landed on Earth again.'

Ian pushed his way through the bushes, holding them back for the girl to follow him, and together they wandered a few paces through the trees.

Barbara said, 'Have you ever thought what you'd do, Ian, if the Doctor landed us back in our own time in England?'

He looked at the sunlight filtering through the trees above their heads, occasionally catching in her eyes as they walked. It was a question which had often occurred to him, one he had frequently thought of asking her. Before he could answer, a sudden shout broke the silence of the forest, stopping them in their tracks. The word itself meant nothing to them at that particular moment, and it's doubtful if they even realized it gave them the key to where they were on Earth and the period of its history. All they did know was that the sound was the beginning of danger, of trouble.

'Saladin!'

The one word pierced out of the silence and hung around them in the short silence that followed. Barbara glanced quickly at the man beside her.

'That wasn't either of you calling, was it?' they heard the Doctor say from the other side of the ring of bushes. Ian took hold of Barbara's hand as other cries and shouts began to ring out from the forest and the sharp ring of metal striking metal.

'We'll get back to the ship,' said Ian.

They were just moving back to the safety of the bushes when a man came running through the trees, a curved sword in his hand. He wore a metal helmet with a long point and a short cape was pinned at the neck and hung behind him. Under the sleeveless breast-plate of small chain metal, a rich dark-blue jacket finished just below his elbows and the rest of the arms were covered with leather wrist protectors studded with metal buttons. A dark-red sash was tied round his waist and the loose, baggy trousers were thrust into soft leather boots with pointed toes. As soon as he saw Ian and Barbara he raised his sword, changed direction slightly and rushed at them, his dark face tightening into fury and hatred.

Ian dropped on one knee and gripped the sword hand of

his new enemy, but fell with him in the power of the man's approaching rush.

'Run, Barbara!' he shouted.

Barbara looked around quickly for a stone or a thick piece of wood to help Ian as the two men rolled and wrestled on the ground. Finally she saw a thick branch some yards away to her left, partially hidden by some bushes. She ran to it and started pulling it out from the grass which had overgrown it. A hand appeared from nowhere, clamped itself around her mouth and pulled her through the bushes, the other arm pinioning itself around her threshing body. Barbara looked up wildly at her captor, who was dressed in a similar fashion to the man with whom Ian was fighting only a few yards away. She kicked out with her legs to try and break the man's hold on her, nearly got free and then slumped to the earth unconscious, as a sharp blow from the man's fist caught her at the base of the neck.

The Doctor and Vicki peered out from the bushes at

Ian's struggles. The soldier had lost his sword by this time, but he had a very good stranglehold on Ian's neck and was doing his best to squeeze life out of him.

'Get me a rock or something, my child,' murmured the Doctor mildly as he watched the fight. Ian managed to break the stranglehold, half rose from beneath the soldier's body, intending to throw him to the ground but fell back as one of the man's leather and metal wristlets smashed into the side of his head, the effort causing the Saracen's helmet to fall off.

'Be careful, Chesterton,' said the Doctor, 'he's going to butt you with his head. Ah! I told you he would.'

The soldier, conscious now that he had a new enemy behind him, was trying to get away from Ian and reach for his sword. The Doctor walked over a few paces and stepped on the sword firmly. Vicki ran up with a small stone and handed it to the Doctor, who weighed it in his hand reflectively.

'Well, don't just stand there,' panted Ian.

'Oh, very well. Hold him still, then.'

Ian rolled so that the soldier lay on top of him and the Doctor stepped nearer and brought the stone down on top of his head sharply. The soldier groaned and rolled away. Ian picked himself up, and Vicki helped him to brush the dirt and leaves from his clothes.

'Thanks very much,' he said, sarcastically. The Doctor suddenly pitched the stone away from him and hurried his two friends into the cover of the ring of bushes as he heard the sound of approaching men.

In a second, they watched as four or five men in simple hunting clothes, obviously retreating through the wood, fought a rearguard action against twice as many soldiers with the pointed helmets. One of the men in hunting clothes was badly wounded, a short arrow sticking out of his body at the top of his right shoulder, the blood coursing down his tunic, the red stain showing up clearly in the dappled sunlight. Another of the hunters fell, an arrow through his heart, while the tallest of the huntsmen, different only from his companions by his head of red-gold hair, fought a violent, hand-to-hand battle with three of the pursuing soldiers, running his sword through one and crashing the hilt on top of another's face. The third, who carried a lance, reversed it suddenly and swung it in an arc. The end of it just struck the top of the red-headed giant's forehead. With a roar of rage and pain, he fell into some bushes and disappeared from sight.

'We ought to help them,' said Ian urgently, but the Doctor held on to Ian's arm.

'Think of the women, Chesterton! We must hold ourselves ready to defend them.'

'Yes, Barbara's hiding somewhere on the other side of those trees,' murmured Ian, with an anxious frown.

Suddenly the fighting stopped and one of the huntsmen, the only one left standing, held up his arms as four of the soldiers made to run at him.

'I am Malec Ric,' he shouted.

A man pushed his way through the small ring of soldiers and approached the huntsman.

'You have no friends to protect you now, Malec Ric.' The huntsman looked slowly around the wood, his eyes moving from first one and then another of his friends lying on the ground.

'I am the Emir, El Akir,' continued the man with the scar.

'Am I to die as well?' said the man at bay. 'If so dispatch me and have done with it.'

El Akir shook his head slowly, a cruel smile twisting his lips.

'Your fate will be decided elsewhere. To tell of killing the English King, Malec Ric, is a vain story that only a fool might invent. To show a *captured* Malec Ric is what El Akir shall do.'

23

The tall huntsman stared at the Emir coldly. 'Take me then and leave my friends in peace.'

'A king at liberty may give commands. A captured one obeys them.'

He gestured sharply to the soldiers and the prisoner was hustled away by two of them. A look of utter satisfaction filled El Akir's face, as he beckoned up another of the soldiers to his side.

'Take such men as you need, search out the others and kill them,' he commanded. The soldier bowed his head and the Emir walked away, following the soldiers who were now disappearing through the trees with their prisoner.

As soon as he was left alone, the soldier began to beat in the bushes with the flat side of his sword, searching for any hidden enemies. Another soldier appeared and did the same thing.

Vicki suddenly realized that her foot was showing through the bushes. Before she could draw it out of sight, one of the soldiers spotted her, thrust a hand through the foliage and dragged her out into view. Ian immediately launched himself out of his cover, while the Doctor picked up a discarded lance and beat off the approach of the second soldier. Once again the wood resounded with the sound of conflict, but this time the contest was considerably more uneven than before. The Doctor's lance was no match for the curved sword and all he could do was thrust and parry desperately, while Ian found himself up against a strong opponent, and without any weapon at all.

One of the wounded men in hunting clothes, Sir William de Tornebu, still weak from the arrow wound in his shoulder, pulled himself to his knees and signalled to Vicki, who ran over to him. He was struggling to draw the sword that hung at his side and she pulled it out for him. He gestured her gently, but firmly, to one side, held the sword lightly as if it were a javelin and threw it with all the strength he could muster, falling to the ground with the effort.

The sword flashed through the air and struck at the soldier who had pinned Ian against a tree. It buried itself deeply into his back, just as he was raising his sword to cut Ian in half. For a second or two the soldier stood, his weapon raised in his hand, a look of absolute surprise on his face. Then he staggered and fell to one side, the sword slipping out of his nerveless hand. Ian picked it up and ran over to where the Doctor was engaged with the other Saracen and, after a few short strokes, ended the matter finally with a fierce cut as the soldier's guard dropped. Ian threw the sword away from him and walked with the Doctor to where Vicki was trying to nurse de Tornebu, whose effort had expended his last reserve of energy. He lay in Vicki's arms, his eyes closed.

'We have our friend here to thank for our lives,' said the Doctor seriously, bending beside the injured man. 'These Saracens would have killed all of us without a second's thought.'

'Saracens!' echoed Ian.

'Of course. You heard that man announcing himself as "Malec Ric", didn't you? That was what the Saracens called King Richard of England.'

'Richard the Lionheart,' added Vicki. The man in her arms opened his eyes and looked up at the three people around him weakly. It was obvious that even the effort of keeping his eyelids open was a strain.

'Not . . . not the King,' he muttered. The Doctor bent down on one knee.

'What was that, my friend?'

'The man . . . who called himself Malec Ric . . .' the other gasped, 'was Sir . . . Sir William des Preaux. The King . . . if he lives . . . give him the . . . belt.'

De Tornebu's head fell back again.

Vicki said : 'Is he dead?'

The Doctor shook his head. 'No, but he's badly wounded. We must take that arrow out.'

25

'What did he mean about the belt?' asked Vicki. She searched inside a pouch belonging to the unconscious man, pulled out a jewel-encrusted gold belt and gasped in astonishment.

'Gold . . . and rubies. Diamonds too, Doctor.'

'Very useful,' murmured the Doctor thoughtfully. He suddenly looked up. 'Where's Chesterton gone?'

Ian suddenly came running towards them.

'I can't find Barbara anywhere,' he cried. 'I thought she must have hidden when the fight started, but she isn't anywhere.'

The Doctor looked at the young man seriously, then down at the ornate belt in his hand.

'I'm afraid it looks as if the Saracens have taken her,' he said quietly. There was a pause for a moment or two, then Ian reached down and picked up a sword from the ground.

'What do you think you're going to do?'

'Go after her, of course,' Ian said.

'Don't be a fool,' said the Doctor sharply. 'We're in an enemy country and surrounded by huge armies. You'd be outnumbered thousands to one. Try to be sensible, I beg of you.'

Ian pressed his lips together stubbornly and started to argue with the Doctor. For a moment, Vicki thought they'd come to blows, as the older of the two men stood up, his fists clenched and his whole body shaking with rage.

Ian, almost beside himself with anxiety, tried to ignore what he knew was sound advice, but eventually realized he couldn't possibly succeed by throwing himself after Barbara. He looked at the sword in his hand disgustedly, broke it over his knee and threw the two pieces as far away from him as he could. The Doctor put a hand on his shoulder sympathetically.

'We all have the same wish, Chesterton. I have a plan to achieve Barbara's return, too. We have this wounded knight here, and we have this valuable piece of jewellery.' He held

27

up the golden belt, and the sunlight brought out all the facets of the jewels embedded in it, until it dazzled the eye with its richness and beauty.

'How can they help us?'

'We shall take both the knight and the golden belt to King Richard,' stated the Doctor. 'He will be in our debt. He will then accede to your request to go after Barbara, to the court of Saladin, and arrange for her release. It's the only way, my boy, believe me.'

Ian turned the plan over in his mind and then, after a few seconds, he agreed with it. The Doctor patted him on the back in satisfaction.

'Good. Now you're being intelligent. But can you also be patient?'

'Why?'

The Doctor spread out his hands.

'We can't possibly go to King Richard wearing clothes like these. We are on Earth at the time of the Third Crusade, my boy, in Palestine; some time between A.D. 1190 and 1192. We must find wearing apparel suitable to the time and place.'

'Haven't you anything in the ship?' demanded Ian.

The Doctor shook his head. 'Worse than that, my boy, I have no money either. However, it can't be very far to the town where Richard has his headquarters. I will go there and find a way to get us something to wear. You and Vicki must wait here and look after this wounded man.'

Ian stared at him stubbornly for a few moments. The Doctor read all the doubt and anxiety in his eyes and knew that the younger man was matching this against all those other times when the Doctor's advice had been the wiser course of action. Eventually, Ian nodded and turned away.

'Fetch my long, black cloak from the ship, will you, my child?' murmured the Doctor.

Vicky ran away and disappeared through the screen of bushes. The Doctor rested a hand lightly on Ian's arm.

'We will find her.'

'You're so sure. So certain. Doctor, we've lived on a knife-edge. We can't go on and on relying on luck and good fortune!'

'Do you really believe that's what it's been?' The Doctor shook his head. 'Frankly, I never rely on luck. A most dangerous occupation. No, my boy, I believe in positive thought. I believe in optimism, provided one never takes it to ridiculous lengths. But above all, Chesterton, I'm convinced in the strength of logic and reasoned action. Impulse is all right in a fight, when the odds are against you and only some brilliant piece of improvisation can turn defeat into victory.'

'Maybe.' Ian managed a smile. 'You're usually right.'

The Doctor chuckled and took the robe from Vicki as she returned. He moved off, saying over his shoulder, 'Now keep under cover. Possess yourselves in patience. The old Doctor will find a way.'

As soon as the Doctor disappeared through the trees, the long cloak huddled around him to disguise the rest of his clothes, Ian felt all his worry returning. It was exactly at moments like these when he was very like the Ian Chesterton of old; unsure of himself, frustrated with inactivity, his fertile imagination working overtime as he pictured Barbara in the hands of the Saracens, and particularly a prisoner of the man with the scar, who had called himself El Akir.

At that very moment, Barbara was being carried out of the forest bound uncomfortably to a horse, her wrists and legs tied to each other under the stomach of the animal, dizzy from the blood running into her head as she hung downwards.

'Who is the English woman?' she heard one of the soldiers say, who rode near her.

'I do not know,' another replied. 'Nor do I know why we waste our time taking her to Ramlah.'

'Oh, she will fetch something in the slave market,' said the first soldier.

Barbara closed her eyes, a dead weight of fear pressing in on her. Her head swam and she felt consciousness slipping away from her. As if from a long way away, she heard one of the soldiers speaking again.

'Perhaps she will be useful as an entertainment for El Akir. They say he has a hundred ways to torture slowly.'

And as the two soldiers laughed together, the merciful oblivion of unconsciousness stole over Barbara, blotting out everything around her in a jet-black cloud of forgetfulness.

CHAPTER TWO

The Knight of Jaffa

'The less said about the Doctor, the better,' Barbara had once said to Ian in the ship, after a particularly dangerous adventure. 'It's his constant air of mystery that makes him what he is.'

The Doctor hadn't overheard this remark, but it would have delighted him if he had. It was the Doctor's very personal and peculiar strain of individuality that made him capable of bridging all the different places he visited, accepting them on their own terms. He would land abruptly in a new world as a stranger and yet, all at once, become a part of that world; reaching out with curiosity and friendly interest to such a great degree that people assumed him to be no more than an ordinary visitor from across a range of mountains, or from over a small sea.

Thus it was in the town of Jaffa, where the Doctor quickly found his way to the merchant houses and shops, where he knew he could find the vital clothes he and his friends needed.

As he strolled through the town, careful to observe as many of the local customs as he could, noting every action of the other passers-by, so that he would commit no offence or give himself away, he might very well have been an old man walking in the early evening, sightseeing perhaps, or a deeply religious person wearing the simplest of clothes to mark his attitude to life. Around him, the busy little town, prospering with the settlement of King Richard's armies, flourished and developed. It attracted all sorts of people from a dozen and one countries. Groups of strolling players followed the army, earning purses of gold for their song singing and acting stories of the ancient Greek heroes. Many teams of sinuous dancing girls, from Circassia, Greece, India and Persia, some as dark as shadows and with tiny bells on their slender ankles and wrists, tempted all to watch them. Musicians filled the streets with melodies, tumblers and acrobats delighted the eye with their speed and dexterity. Sailors from the ships in the harbour drank the local wine of Jaffa and added laughter to the many other sounds. Merchants from Pisa, Venice and Genoa talked and treated, traded and made bargains and most of all, in all this motley mass of humanity, the fighting men from Europe mingled in and were the greatest number. Fine-nosed Austrians, strong-jawed Germans and well-set Frenchmen all laughed and walked, drank and talked with the men of Kent, Cornishmen, Welshmen, men from Yorkshire and Lancashire, the Englishmen who called Richard their King.

Small wonder that the Doctor went unnoticed in this seething mass of humanity and, although he blessed the crowds for the cover they provided, it was, nevertheless, with a sigh of relief that he turned into a quieter street and set his sights upon the shop of one Ben Daheer. The trader stood talking to an English soldier as the Doctor made his unobtrusive way towards the two stalls which flanked the entrance, both loaded with bales of silks and satins. It was obvious to the Doctor that the two men were having some sort of argument, although it was conducted in undertones.

'Thatcher,' said Ben Daheer, with a shake of his plump little face, 'these clothes you bring me are difficult to sell.'

The soldier pushed his sullen face close to the shop-owner's, and bared his yellow teeth unpleasantly.

'I took a chance fetching these things,' he grated. 'There's twice as much as I brought last time. Yet you offer me half as much!'

'If you are not satisfied, take the clothes back.'

'You know I can't do that, you fat villain!'

Ben Daheer pretended not to hear the insult. He opened his pouch at his waist and counted out a few coins into Thatcher's greedy hands.

'That's all they're worth to me. Complain to the people you stole the clothes from.'

The two men stared at each other, the one angry, the other calm. Then Thatcher slouched away, muttering under his breath. Ben Daheer turned to go inside his shop with the clothes under his arm and spotted the Doctor.

'Ah! Am I not looked upon with favour,' he breathed, his fat little body shaking with pleasure. 'Of course you are from Pisa, My Lord?'

The Doctor peered at Ben Daheer, with a slight smile on his face.

'No.'

'Genoa, then?'

'I know the place.'

'Ah, you traders from Venice are cautious.'

'I am not Venetian. And I am not a trader.'

Ben Daheer bowed as low as the clothes under his arm and his considerable girth allowed him.

'Your pardon, My Lord, the richness of your cloak is hidden by the darkness.'

'You have some fine materials here,' murmured the Doctor.

'The finest in Jaffa, My Lord.'

'That's what they all say.'

Ben Daheer laid a persuasive hand on the Doctor's arm and urged him inside the shop, laying down the bundle of stolen clothes he had bought on a table just inside the entrance.

'My Lord,' he said earnestly, 'a man with nine sons and two daughters has too many mouths to feed to tell lies. Examine my goods. Baghdad, Basrah, Persia. Silk, satin, cloths of all kinds and all colours.'

The Doctor looked about him keenly and noticed the figure of a tall, well-dressed man examining a roll of silk. The man had an arrogance about him, a proud set to his head, and a pair of black eyes which gave the Doctor a cursory glance, and then dismissed him.

'Serve your other client,' murmured the Doctor, 'and I will search for what I want.'

Ben Daheer bowed and moved away. The Doctor waited until both backs were turned to him, then bent down on his knees and scuttled under the table beside the door, pulling and arranging a piece of hanging cloth to hide him from view.

'Now, honourable master, how may I serve you,' said Ben Daheer, rubbing his hands together. The taller man turned from his contemplation of a bale of particularly fine silk, his black eyes piercing into those of the fat little shop-owner.

'I am Luigi Ferrigo, merchant of Genoa. I am in Jaffa to buy and sell.'

Ben Daheer turned away thoughtfully, assessing the meaning of the words. He did not want to lose a potential customer, but he didn't want to encourage a salesman. As if divining his thoughts, the Genoese laughed lightly.

'I have it in my mind to buy from you, Ben Daheer. I like the quality of your goods. I can dispose of your entire stock of cloth in Genoa, ten times over.'

Ben Daheer was so excited, Ferrigo so intent, that neither of them noticed the hand which crept out from beneath a small table beside the entrance. The hand reached up as far as it could to the clothes heaped upon the table top, fingering and sampling until it came into contact with a cloth it liked. With a swift jerk the hand pulled and some clothes disappeared.

'My Lord, this is exhilarating news,' cried Ben Daheer, almost wriggling with delight.

'However,' interrupted the Genoese seriously, 'one thing stands in our way.'

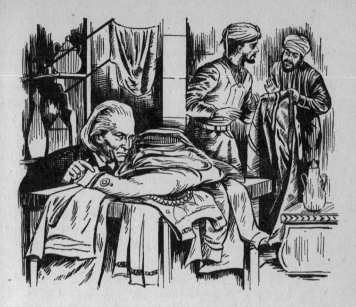

The shopkeeper was so attracted to the use of the word
'our', with its suggestion of partnership and future riches,
that he gripped hold of Ferrigo's sleeve urgently.

'Nothing is too difficult. How can I help?'

The other man detached the hand from his sleeve gently
and moved a little into the shadows. Ben Daheer followed
eagerly, anxious to close what seemed to him to be a won-
derful business deal. Again, neither of the men noticed the
hand appearing and disappearing rapidly, or realized that
the bundle of clothes recently acquired by Ben Daheer was
rapidly diminishing. Had either of them possessed ultra-
keen hearing, they might just have detected a soft chuckle
emanating from beneath the little table by the doorway.
But, fortunately for the Doctor, they were each too heavily
engaged in their business talk, and the wily old man, satisfied now with the clothes he had acquired, was busily
wrapping them around his body underneath his cloak.

'I must talk with the Sultan,' said Ferrigo, after a pause. Ben Daheer stared at him in bewilderment.

'The Sultan?'

'Saladin.'

Ben Daheer stepped back, his face betraying nervousness, his hands clenching and unclenching by his side. He looked around him nervously.

'Hush, I implore you,' he stuttered. 'Do you not realize that his enemies are everywhere in Jaffa? To talk of the Sultan so openly would bring ruin on both of us. Why, the English King's palace is no more than a short step from here . . .'

'And a glittering fortune is near your hands,' interposed Ferrigo. 'I need a horse and a guide. And an assurance I may pass through to the Sultan without harm to my person or my possessions.'

'My Lord, it is impossible. I am afraid . . .'

Luigi Ferrigo turned and walked towards the doorway.

'Arrange for me to travel to see the Sultan and I shall make you a rich man. I shall return in one hour for your answer, Ben Daheer.'

Ben Daheer ran after the Genoese, following him out a little way into the street, confused and bewildered by the rapidity of the conversation. Avarice quarrelled with fear and all of the little shopkeeper's emotions showed on his face as he turned back into his shop again, his brain working overtime, testing this idea, trying this one, abandoning another, until his head ached. He was so busy wondering and worrying that he cannoned into the Doctor and, with a little squeal of fear, nearly fell to his knees, afraid that his recent conversation had been overheard.

'Well, my friend,' smiled the Doctor, 'I fear I do not find quite what I want to buy.'

'Have you been here all this time?' stammered Ben Daheer.

'Yes, examining this and that. Did you make a sale to

your other customer? I did not hear what passed between you.'

Ben Daheer's body stopped quivering and he even managed a half-smile.

'We may do business, he and I. I am sorry nothing pleases you here.'

'Ah, but I am pleased. And I have to thank you very much.'

Ben Daheer looked at the Doctor suspiciously.

'Thank me? What for?'

'For being here, my friend. When you were most needed. And one day I shall find a way to reward you.'

He turned and walked out of the shop, leaving Ben Daheer with his temptation and his fear.

The story of how the Doctor acquired clothes for himself, Ian and Vicki, and what had transpired between the shop-keeper and the mysterious Genoese merchant enlivened the difficult affair of transporting the wounded knight, Sir William de Tornebu, from the little forest to Jaffa. The Doctor found, on his return to his two friends, that Ian had constructed a rough stretcher of branches and that Vicki had patiently bathed and dressed the knight's shoulder wound, after having helped Ian to draw the arrow. He learned that the knight had suffered a slight fever, recovered from it and was now able to sleep peacefully, although his waking moments were so few and far between it gave them some concern. The Doctor owed his title more to science than medicine but was, nevertheless, able to satisfy himself that the wounded man was on the road to recovery and could withstand the uncomfortable journey to Jaffa.

Their reception there was immediate and popular. Dressed in the clothes – which the Doctor insisted he had only 'borrowed' – from Ben Daheer's shop, Ian now wore a simple hunting habit, soft leather breeches and calf-length boots, and a russet-coloured tunic belted at the waist. The

Doctor wore a long robe of quiet design, with a rather ornate collar fastened high on the neck and covering his shoulders. Vicki was dressed as a page, with long, dark-blue tights and pointed ankle-high shoes, an extremely smart long-sleeve yellow vest and, over it, a thigh-length grey tunic with short puffed sleeves. Ian was convinced that as soon as they came in sight of the people of Jaffa they would be pointed at, seized as spies or impostors and pushed into the nearest dungeon to await an early death, but he soon found out that there were many others dressed in similar fashion and that, rather than being rushed off to prison, the three of them were hailed by soldiers and civilians alike as heroes for bringing in a wounded knight, saving him from wandering bands of thieves or discovery by roaming Saracen patrols.

The Doctor immediately demanded to be taken before King Richard, and found, as he guessed he would, an immediate way through the various courtiers and advisers, where, in any ordinary event, the three of them might have kicked their heels in frustration for days.

It was some five hours since the fight in the wood and they were shown into a lofty stone room in Richard's headquarters to find him suffering the rather ungentle hands of a physician, who was attempting to clean a deep cut on the King's forehead. He sat in his chair, wincing as he listened to the three strangers being introduced by their guide, the Earl of Leicester. Leicester had a notable name as a fighting man, having on many occasions stood by Richard's side and helped him fight through small armies of the enemy. He was a compact, tough warrior, averse to fancy speeches and embroidered compliments. He told the King simply that three heroes deserved his attention, indicated to servants to bring in the body of the wounded knight on the rough stretcher, bowed and withdrew.

Richard ran his eyes over the Doctor and his two companions and pushed himself away from his chair.

'Enough, enough,' he growled, wiping the water from his face. The physician bowed and hurried away and the King walked over to the stretcher and stared down at Sir William de Tornebu, who was now awake.

'Forgive me for not rising, Sire,' he whispered.

'Rest yourself. Tell me, if you can summon up the strength, what happened in the wood? A blow on the head sent me staggering into the bushes. I came to my senses and crawled away, lucky to find a riderless horse, too dazed to know who I was or where, until the walls of Jaffa cleared the mist from my mind.'

De Tornebu related the events of the ambush and how Sir William des Preaux had gallantly declared himself as the King in order that Richard might be given time to escape.

'And I was too injured to know much more,' he continued, 'except that these kindly people saved my life and brought me here.' De Tornebu drifted off into sleep again.

The King nodded and turned to walk back to his throne.

'Good friends indeed. We thank you.'

The Doctor bowed slightly as the King seated himself.

'The brothers L'Etable dead,' murmured the King, 'and de Marun. Sir William des Preaux taken. What have I left from my foolish hunting sortie but one wounded friend and a sore head?'

The Doctor stepped forward.

'One small thing remains yours, Sire,' he remarked, opening a pouch at his belt and drawing out the jewel-encrusted golden belt. Richard took it from him and weighed it in his hand thoughtfully.

'You are honest as well as brave, and again we thank you. But I'd change this for de Marun and the others.'

He suddenly threw the belt angrily away from him and it flew, sparkling and flashing through the air, skidded along the stone floor and lay, half hidden, in the fresh rushes that carpeted the room.

'Friends cut down about my ears, or stolen! My armies roust about and clutter up the streets of Jaffa with the garbage of their vices. And an hour ago I learn that John, my brother, finds a thirst for power in England; drinking great draughts of it, although it is not his to take. He's planning to usurp my throne, and so trades with my enemy, Philip of France! A tragedy of fortunes and I'm too much beset by them. A curse on this day! A thousand curses!'

Richard hammered his fist on his knee in fury and turned his head aside. The Doctor drew the others away slightly.

'We must ask him about Barbara,' Ian said.

'I'm not sure this is the right time,' murmured the Doctor. 'Oughtn't we to wait until he's in a better mood, my boy?'

'We can't wait any longer. This was your idea, Doctor, to get the King to help us.'

The Doctor shrugged and Ian moved to the silent man on his throne, alone with his troubles. He looked up as Ian bowed, his face clearing slightly.

'Sire, there were four of us in that wood. Our other companion, a lady, was stolen by the Saracens. We assume she was held prisoner like Sir William des Preaux, destined for Saladin's court.'

Richard nodded slowly as he listened, but it was obvious to Ian that his thoughts were elsewhere.

'I am most sorry,' he said vaguely, 'but I must ask you not to bother me with such things now.'

'I am only asking you,' said Ian firmly, 'to give me escort to Saladin's headquarters.'

'And what do you do when you are there?'

'Arrange for the lady's release. Perhaps bring back Sir William des Preaux, if I can.'

'As my emissary to Saladin?'

'Yes.'

'Pay him compliments, give him something in return for his benevolence?'

The Doctor moved forward.

'He can hardly have much use for a player King and a young woman, Your Majesty.'

Richard shook his head definitely.

'I will not do it.'

'But I can get them back,' insisted Ian.

'No!'

'All I need is . . .'

'Are you deaf?' shouted the King. 'We do not trade with Saladin today. Not today, tomorrow nor any day henceforth.'

There was a short silence as Ian and the Doctor looked at each other. The Doctor patted Ian's arm reassuringly and tried to reopen the discussion.

'King Richard, I beg of you to listen to us. Our friend is just a woman, unused to the ways of fighting men and war.'

If the Doctor was conscious of his untruth, he showed no sign of it on his face.

'A gentle, sweet-natured girl,' he continued persuasively, 'surely not destined for rough handling by hordes of fighting men. Certainly not meant to be frightened, perhaps tortured, and put to death. Have pity on her, Sire. Let us help her.'

Richard obviously responded to the Doctor's call for chivalry. Before he could answer, however, de Tornebu, who had fallen into a rather uneasy sleep, must have moved on the stretcher, putting pressure on his wounded shoulder. A groan issued out of his lips and made the King forget what he was about to say. All he remembered was the ambush in the forest. Worse, he remembered the warning of Sir William des Preaux, which had fallen on such stony ground.

White with fury, mostly aimed at his own shortsightedness and obstinacy, Richard swung round and pointed a finger at the Doctor.

'Understand this,' he shouted. 'I'll not trade with the man who killed my friends!'

CHAPTER THREE

A New Scheherazade

There was a long silence. The King lay back in his cere-
monial chair, lost in anger and frustration, brooding over
the misfortunes of the day. The Doctor's head was bent
down, his eyes searching the ground, as if he would find the
answer to the impasse there among the rushes covering the
worn stone. Ian felt the ultimate in despair, his confidence
deserting him, making him a prey to all the doubts and fears
about Barbara he had so successfully pushed to one side,
in the belief Richard would help. He hardly felt Vicki put
a hand on his arm, scarcely saw the sympathy in her eyes.
He only knew that the woman he loved was far away, in
dangerous hands, while he was absolutely powerless to save
her.

'A very proper attitude, Your Majesty,' murmured the
Doctor, so mildly that the King darted a look at him to see
if he was being sarcastic. 'If you want Saladin to score over
you,' he continued.

'What do you mean by that?' snapped Richard.

'I mean, Sire, that in your understandable rage you are
ignoring a chance to make Saladin look foolish. It may seem
to you that you left a little of your pride in that wood. But I
assure you there's capital to be made of this affair. Besides
the violence and tragedy, it has a humorous side.'

Richard stared at the Doctor as if he were mad.

'Humour!'

'Indeed. Here's Saladin, mighty ruler, commander of

huge armies. A troop of his soldiers is sent to capture you; and what happens? He ends up with one of your knights and a young lady.'

Ian, shaken now out of his torpor, appreciated the new line the Doctor was taking and moved to his side.

'You could turn this into a good story against Saladin,' he said eagerly.

'A troop of men to capture one knight!' exclaimed the Doctor. 'Why he'd need an army by itself to capture your horse!'

'You could have this story spread by word of mouth,' added Ian. 'Have songs sung, actors perform plays about it. All this country would suspect that Saladin fears you so much, he spends his time on foolish plots.'

'And when you'd done all that,' said the Doctor calmly, noting the slight smile beginning to appear on Richard's lips, 'you could send to Saladin and ask him if he'd finished playing games, and could you have your knight back.'

Richard suddenly put back his head and roared with laughter.

'There is a jest here,' he said at last, shaking his head. 'A grim one with our friends dead, but Saladin must be as much put out by this affair as I am.'

Richard stood up and put an arm around the Doctor's shoulders.

'By my father's name, you have wit, old man. We are conscious of the service you have rendered and will like to see you here in court. As to the sending of a messenger, let me think on it. I must find a reason other than an exchange of prisoners, or Saladin will believe they are too important to me.'

'Very gracious of you, Your Majesty,' murmured the Doctor.

At that moment, a girl swept into the room, and Richard's eyes softened as he went to meet her.

'Richard, are you wounded?' she cried anxiously.

Richard took both her hands, shaking his head.

'A graze, no more. But meet with new friends, Joanna. Courage, bravery and wit are gathered here.'

Joanna stood beside her brother and acknowledged the bows gracefully with a delightful smile, always happy to meet anyone who held Richard's admiration. She stood no higher than his shoulder and her long, fair hair hung down her back in a cascade of beauty. Ian could scarcely take his eyes off such a vision of perfection, who earned for herself no more than a few lines in the history books he had read. Her finely sculptured face, with its high cheek-bones and wide generous mouth, the delicate ivory of her skin, just faintly tinged with colour at the cheeks, the classically simple gown that emphasized the perfect proportions of her figure, all made an impact on him he knew he would never forget.

Joanna moved from her brother's side to where de Tornebu lay.

'This man is losing blood. Why, it is Sir William de Tornebu, Richard. I heard you had been fighting, but did not know your friend was injured.'

The King clapped his hands together twice in summons. 'I will have the Chamberlain take care of him.'

The Chamberlain entered the room, a tall, dignified figure, so imposing in his clothes and manner that, to Vicki's eyes, he almost rivalled the King.

'Chamberlain, take this knight and see his wounds are cared for. Find places for these three friends. And note, they have my patronage.'

The Chamberlain bowed, signalled for attendants to take Sir William away and then turned to the Doctor, waving a hand in a most regal fashion.

As he smiled at each of them in turn, his face became more and more bewildered and finally, as he ran his eyes over Vicki's clothes, his bewilderment turned to a heavy frown of concentration. The King touched him impatiently on the shoulder.

'Go about your business, Chamberlain! Why do you stand here gaping? Be off with you, man, and see our friends have every comfort.'

The Chamberlain shook himself out of his wonderment, convinced now that there was something distinctly familiar about the clothes these new companions of the King wore. Putting the mystery aside, he gestured grandly with his hands, requesting that they follow him and, bowing to the King and Joanna, left the room.

'Go with him,' said the King. 'Come to me in a while, when you have eaten and rested.'

As soon as they disappeared, Joanna linked arms with her brother and walked with him through the room, down a short corridor which opened out on to a terrace. They talked of Berengaria, Richard's wife, who was in the city of Acre, which he considered safer for her than Jaffa, only so recently captured. They looked out from the terrace over the rooftops of the busy little town and watched the proud ships that cluttered the harbour. It was then that Richard noticed a fine jewel strung around the girl's neck by a golden strand and asked her where she had bought it.

'Oh, this is a strange gift, Richard,' she laughed. 'From the men you fight.'

'Saladin?' exclaimed Richard.

'No, his brother, Saphadin. I have given him no cause for such attentions,' she went on hurriedly, as she saw her brother's eyes darken. Richard shook his head in amazement.

'Saladin sends me presents of fruit and snow. When I was so ill, no kinder words were sent to me than his. Now his brother decorates you with his jewels.'

He looked out across the sea, the young man who had brought the armies of Europe half-way across the civilized world, the only man those armies would really follow and die for, if he commanded it. In the ten years of his reign as King of England that country would be his home for only a few short months and he was destined to die before his time, in a foreign country. Now, Richard, at thirty-four, a mixture of a man, whose fearless courage on the battlefield was admired by friend and foe, yet who could be moved to tears by music, wrestled with the problem of his enemy's strange behaviour.

'These men oppose us,' he said. 'These courtesies they do us. I am confused by their soft words, when all at once our armies lock in deadly combat; watering the land with a rain of blood, and the thunder in the skies is deafened by the shouts of dying men.'

'Your heart calls for England, Richard.'

'Aye, it does.'

'Is there no sort of peace with Saladin?'

Richard didn't answer her. His eyes had just fallen idly on the jewel around her neck, noticing the girl's fingers playing with it at her throat. It was a rare stone, beautifully set, the sort given by a man enamoured of a woman, who hoped such a present might soften her heart and force her to listen carefully to what an ardent man might have to say. As he stared at it, assessing its worth and calculating the reason for the giving of it, Richard suddenly realized it provided him with a key to unlock a door he had long desired to open. The way to a peaceful settlement of the war with Saladin. As if to lend force to the argument, Joanna spoke again.

'You should try and settle with the Sultan, Richard. The armies have fought well but many, so many, have died. And remember that John rules for you in England now. He is not to be trusted, as well you know.'

Richard smiled at his sister and put an arm round her slender waist.

'I promise you, beauty, I shall try and find a common meeting-ground with Saladin. Now, we have had our little talk and I have business to get under way.'

'So I'm to be packed off, am I?' she demanded, her eyes catching fire in the sun, her chin thrusting out a little.

'Aye, packed off and beaten first, if you don't behave,' he growled ferociously. She suddenly laughed and ran away from him into the building, her long hair streaming behind her, her little jewelled slippers tapping over the stones and rustling the reeds.

Richard returned to his state-room, commanded the three strangers to be brought before him and ordered that a monk be found and conducted to the room, as well as the means of writing.

The Doctor, Ian and Vicki, who had spent their time pleasantly enough exploring the palace, found the King dictating a letter. He waved them into the room where they stood silently as he spoke to a monk bending low over the parchment spread out on a small table.

'And, not only this kingdom, its fortresses and towns shall be yours,' said Richard, 'but all the Frankish kingdom. My sister, Joanna, ex-queen of Sicily, whose beauty is already talked of wherever men of judgement and discernment are, is a proper match for one who not only rejoices in so grand . . . wait . . .'

The monk looked up expectantly.

'Ah, I have it. In so eminent a brother, as is the Sultan Saladin, but who possesses an eminence of his own. Prince Saphadin, I beg of you to prefer this match between yourself and my sister, and thus make me your brother.'

The King waited until the monk had completed the letter, read the contents aloud and then held the parchment for him to press down his ring upon it.

'See that this is taken immediately,' he ordered, 'with the finest horse you can find as its accompanying gift.'

The monk bowed and hurried from the room, clutching the parchment to his breast as if his whole life depended on it.

'The monk I trust as I would myself,' observed Richard significantly. 'I hope I may rely upon you not to speak of what you have heard?'

The Doctor spread out his hands eloquently.

'Your Majesty, we are deaf and dumb, until you say otherwise.'

'Very well. You see my plan, for it is important you should know of it. Prince Saphadin, the Sultan's brother, is ambitious. He has set his cap for my sister. The marriage terms are peace.'

The Doctor nodded.

'Now you, sirrah,' Richard remarked, gazing at Ian, 'have reason to journey to the Sultan. When you arrive, my letter will have been delivered. You will be in the best position to see what reaction it has, and yet not be suspect. Is Saphadin sincere? Is there a real chance of peace? These are the two questions I shall ask you on your return, and I trust you may be able to answer them.'

Ian was so overcome that the King had turned from his former obstinacy that he could only stammer he would do as much as he could.

Richard nodded.

'But you shall go properly, as my emissary.'

'May I leave at once?' demanded Ian.

'I see my hospitality is such here that you cannot wait to get away,' the King smiled. 'Boy, bring me down that sword.'

Vicki, remembering her role as page-boy, ran to a wall upon which was hung a heavy sword and brought it to the throne, bowing low as she presented it. Ian looked bewildered, not understanding what was to happen to him.

'What is your name?' asked the King.

'Ian Chesterton, Sire . . . but . . .'

The Doctor whispered urgently into his ear, pressing down on his arm.

'Kneel down, my boy, kneel down!'

Ian did as the Doctor urged him to do and Richard stepped forward with the sword in his right hand. The Doctor moved away and stood with Vicki, watching the ceremony, as the King in a simple, unaffected way, touched Ian with the sword.

'I, Richard, King of England, by the grace of God . . .'

Ian raised his eyes and looked up at the King as he spoke the words over his head, suddenly and sharply aware of the extraordinary turn of fate which had plucked him away from his own time and chosen to set him down at another to receive the honour. Yet, conscious as he was of the incredibility of it, and of the wide gulf that separated him from the man before whom he knelt, still the tremendous weight of the occasion bore down on him making his heart beat fast and drying his throat. Then he realized that Richard had stopped and was laying down the sword, holding out his hand. Ian pressed his lips to it and felt the King lift him up to his feet.

'Rise up, Sir Ian, Knight of Jaffa,' said Richard. 'You shall be my man, be chivalrous and brave. But most of all,' he went on, his eyes twinkling with humour, 'keep my secret.'

Ian inclined his head, almost lost for words and only just remembering to stumble out some words of gratitude.

'No more speeches,' said the King firmly. 'Go to Saladin. Bring back this lady, and Sir William if you can. And bring me news.'

Ian bowed, gripped the Doctor's hand, smiled at Vicki and walked out of the room, every fresh step sharpening the picture he had of Barbara in his mind, refusing to admit he might not find her, relieved at last that the search had begun.

When Barbara came to her senses, she found herself in a small ante-chamber, lying on top of some rugs laid on a long seat. She raised herself up on one elbow and gazed out of a window made up of many beautifully-carved arches which looked down on to a courtyard. She was not in a position to see much of what was happening below her, but the sounds of men and horses floated upwards. She glanced round the room and saw a tall man with dark hair talking to a woman by one of the arched entrances to the room. Beyond them, the impassive figure of a huge Negro stood, naked to the waist, a thick curved sword held across his shoulder, blade uppermost, his arms folded across his chest.

The man in the hunting clothes gave the woman some coins and took a cloak from her. The woman hurried out, passing the guard outside fearfully, who simply turned his massive head to examine her and then resumed his contemplation of the corridor ahead of him. The man walked towards Barbara, the cloak held out in his hands. She started back slightly, uncertainly, then relaxed as the man smiled pleasantly.

'I do you no harm,' he said gently, laying the cloak over her. He sat on the bench beside her, reached down and picked up a simple goblet and a jug and poured out some water and handed it to her, watching her while she drank gratefully.

'I do not know who you are or how you came to be in the wood outside Jaffa. Your clothing is so strange I felt you would like a cloak to cover you.'

Barbara realized how odd her short skirt must appear and felt it better to keep her own counsel, without inventing any excuses which might make things worse. She thanked him for his courtesy and asked him where they were.

'We are at the Sultan Saladin's palace at Ramlah.'

'I expected to wake up in prison. Why are we here?'

The man smiled, adding more water to the goblet.

'As for you, I can make no guess. But I am here as King Richard, leader of the mighty host, the scourge of the Infidel.'

Barbara said, 'Richard had red hair.'

'Had! Still has, if the ruse has worked.'

He told her what had happened in the forest, how the Saracens had ambushed them, how he had seen Richard knocked into some bushes and had seized the opportunity to cause a diversion to allow the King to get away.

'I am Sir William des Preaux, and some smiles will turn to long faces soon, I have no doubt.'

'What happened to . . . the others. In the forest?'

Sir William shrugged. 'I do not know. But I have a hopeful heart and, what is better, a lucky King. And you, who will not say her name? . . .'

'Barbara.'

'I am keen to know why one so gentle puts herself amid the swords and arrows. And your garments are a fashion in themselves.'

'Take me back to that forest, Sir William, and I'll answer all your questions.'

'You ask for the impossible very lightly.'

'Is it so impossible?'

'Today it is. I am the captive of one El Akir, an Emir in Saladin's forces. He believes I am the King and thinks he has won the war for his master. He is puzzled about you, as I am, and means to question you. How can I explain you to them?'

Barbara drank the last of the water and put the goblet down on the floor.

'Let me help you with your pretence,' she suggested. 'Who rides with the King?'

'Berengaria, the Queen, is in Acre. But the Princess!'

He smacked a hand down on the bench delightedly.

'You shall be Joanna, my sister, and support me in my lies. Then we shall truly make El Akir look stupid. To cause disruption among allies is just as good as cutting them in two in battle.'

Barbara said, 'I seem to have found a brother and a title.'

'And a friend.'

'That's a very comforting thought.'

'We will not confuse Saladin,' murmured des Preaux, 'but we will make El Akir lose face.'

'From the look of him, that might be an improvement.'

The knight put back his head and laughed delightedly.

'You appear to be in good spirits,' said a voice from the archway, and they both turned as El Akir strode into the room. His clothes were richer now, particularly a white knee-length coat of satin, edged with gold, and held together at the waist with a belt of finely-worked silver.

'Enjoy yourselves while you may,' he continued, standing in front of them arrogantly. Sir William yawned obviously and El Akir's eyes gleamed for a moment. In a second, he controlled himself, but Barbara recognized in him a dangerous and vicious enemy.

'The Sultan Yusef Salah ed-Din ibn Ayjub has commanded that all prisoners be treated with compassion. Would you not say his wishes have been complied with?'

'I have no complaint for myself,' replied Sir William, 'but the Sultan of Egypt and Syria will not be pleased when he learns of the way my sister has been treated.'

'Your sister?' El Akir looked quickly at Barbara, who had drawn the cloak around her closely.

'Aye, Joanna, widow of William the Second of Sicily; fifth child of Henry the Second of England; Princess of a domain stretching from the Cheviots to the Pyrenees . . .'

'This explains why you were in the forest,' interrupted El Akir, his eyes widening. Barbara could almost see his mind working. Sir William plunged in heavily to the attack, assuming an expression of extreme indignation.

'My sister has been grossly ill-treated,' he stormed. 'Slung over a horse with her hands and feet tied together, to be carried like a sack of flour. Handled roughly by your men, foul rags stuffed in her mouth! Is this the compassion your mighty Sultan speaks of?'

'Enough of this,' snapped the Emir. 'The woman is all of one piece.'

Sir William shot out a hand, gripped hold of El Akir's clothes and twisted the man so that he was nearly on his knees.

'Woman?! Watch your tongue, Saracen.'

In an instant guards came running into the room and the two men were pulled apart. As the guards bent the Englishman's hands behind his back, El Akir stepped forward and slapped him viciously across the face.

'You have no rights, no privileges, nothing except the benevolence of our ruler! But he will not side against me if you are too insolent. Remember, you are a prisoner here, not a free man.' He turned to Barbara and eyed her appreciatively.

'I came to learn your identity. That you are the King's sister bodes well for me. I can serve both the Sultan and Malec el Adil, or Saphadin as you call him. The brother of the Sultan will rejoice to see the woman he has for so long admired. Bring them!'

El Akir turned on his heel and strode out of the room.

Fortune had played no part in his achievements of the past. He was an Emir simply because he had murdered his brother. He had riches because he had stolen them. Behind the man lay a dark trail of evil, without one saving grace, without one worthy deed. Even the scar he carried on his face was an advertisement of one of the worst of his acts, when he had attempted, after he had murdered his brother, to capture the weeping widow, a woman he had envied and desired until the deed of fratricide was no longer simply for the title but just as much for the wife as well. But when he stood before her, his hand still holding the sword of death, telling the grief-stricken girl what he had done and what her future was to be, a sudden horror of him, plus a determination he should suffer for his crime, had made her find a desperate courage. She had seized up a heavy ornament and struck at him with all her passionate anger. Although his servants had run in and thrust their swords into her, as El Akir lay groaning on the ground, she still had strength enough to say he would carry the sign of murderer until the day he died. And now all women were his enemies and El

Akir delighted in enslaving them. So his pleasure, as he strode towards the Sultan's chamber, was great: a woman would be humbled, her pride destroyed, and he would find favour and perhaps the close confidence of Saladin and Saphadin.

He gained admittance to the chamber of the Sultan without delay and found Saphadin examining a map. The room was divided by a heavy silk curtain and behind it the Emir knew Saladin sat, meditating on the disposition of his armies, pondering on strategy and ready to hear without being seen.

'Malec el Adil, I bring good fortune not only for him who rules over us, but for your delight as well.'

Saphadin looked up from the map, rolled it in his hands and walked over to a low couch heavily draped with fine materials. He sat down and gestured with his hand for El Akir to continue.

'My brother hears you as I do.'

'Know then,' said El Akir, raising his voice slightly, 'that I have the instrument to vanquish the invaders from across the seas and bring victory.'

Saladin, sitting on the other side of the curtain, heard the words and moved his head slightly, his interest caught. A man of slight build, with a somewhat melancholy face in repose which entirely altered once he smiled, Saladin was many of the things a leader of men needed to be. His force of personality was tremendous, although he did not fight as Richard Coeur de Lion did, at the head of his men. This was not through cowardice but simply that his position as Sultan of the mighty Moslem army forbade such action. He had simple tastes, with a hatred for coarseness and ostentation. His courts abounded with philosophers and well-read men. He was refined, courteous and generous. Above all, he had a fine sense of humour. None of these things was as important as the undoubted ability he had to command and control the vast armies at his disposal. Syrians, Turks,

Arabs, each nationality divided into different tribes and loyalties, status and rivalry; each commander jealous of his position; every army anxious to gain success in the field.

Saladin's personal position was only secure when his plans led to victory. He knew to the last degree how tenuous his hold was over the Moslem host (collectively called Saracens by the Crusaders) and that is why his fairness, courtesy and refinement, which no insecurity of position could shake, were all the more to be wondered at.

He listened now, fascinated, as El Akir related the events leading up to the encounter in the forest outside Jaffa, his hands pressed together, almost as if in prayer. The arrogant, triumphant voice of the Emir came to the end of his story.

'And so, Prince, I bring you now the result of that skirmish in the wood.' El Akir snapped his fingers and a guard led Sir William des Preaux into the chamber.

'The King of the English, leader of the invaders, Malec Ric,' he stated. Saphadin remained seated on his throne staring at the Knight curiously and El Akir was half disappointed at the effect. 'The Lion is in our cage, Prince,' he pointed out, but still the expected praise did not issue forth from Saphadin's lips.

'This is but one part of it,' went on the Emir, puzzled by the attitude of his superiors. 'Another prize was in that wood, a glittering jewel already sparkling in your eyes, El Adil. This priceless stone I bring to lay before you, as your heart desires.'

Once again he snapped his fingers, and another guard escorted Barbara into the chamber. El Akir moved to her, took her elbow and brought her before Saphadin.

'The sister of the Malec Ric; Joanna is the way they call her. Here for your command.'

Saphadin looked at Barbara impassively and then at Sir William. His eyes moved to the face of the Emir.

'King Richard and his sister, Joanna?'

El Akir said: 'No less.'

'Less than less!' Saphadin spat out viciously, and El Akir stepped back at the fury in the other's voice. 'Who is this creature, this rowdy jackal who yaps at my feet with tales of fortune and success! Not El Akir, trusted captain. It must be some odious devil who has taken his form and sent himself to torment me!'

'My lord ... all I have said is true ...'

'You vile worm, do you think I do not know the face and the form of the Princess Joanna?'

'But they told me ... he said ... she ...' El Akir tailed away, as he realized the trick that had been played on him. He turned and looked at the smiling faces of Sir William and Barbara.

The scar on his face suddenly showed up a livid red as the blood drained away from his face. Dark though the texture of his skin was, it visibly paled and his eyes took on an extraordinary glow of venomous hatred. Before he could utter the thoughts which showed so plainly on his face, Saladin stepped through the curtains.

'It seems you are the victim of a pretty deception,' he murmured. El Akir made his obeisance.

'At least we have the English King,' he replied, and then stared as Saphadin shook his head sorrowfully, and Saladin smiled.

'This is not King Richard,' said Saladin. 'A blacker head of red-gold hair I never saw.' Saladin moved across to Barbara and stared into her eyes, liking the fearless way the girl returned his attention. 'You have the better bargain, brother. She may not be the Princess, but her beauty lights the room.'

El Akir started to speak and Saladin held up a hand sharply, getting the silence he commanded.

'I do not wish to listen to you!' he said scathingly, and then he turned to Sir William, 'but I will hear what you have to say.'

'Mighty Sultan, know that I am Sir William des Preaux and to aid my King's escape I shouted out his name and took his identity. This lady, Your Highness, has no part in this affair, except to aid my pretence. I beg of you to look upon her kindly, whatever fate you have for me.'

Saladin nodded slowly. 'I salute your chivalry, and your words do not go unheeded.'

El Akir stepped forward, plucking at Saladin's sleeve.

'Hear me! Let me make some good. This woman can be made to entertain you. I can have her dance on hot coals, run through a passage made of sharp-tipped swords or any of a hundred ways in my mind, all for your amusement.'

Saladin thought for a second or two and then looked at Barbara gravely.

'What do you say to this?'

Barbara knew she was being tested as a person, and was determined not to hurry her reply. She also knew that Saladin would be disappointed if she begged for mercy, although she felt he probably expected it. Barbara was never one to take the course people anticipated.

'It sounds to me,' she said at last, 'like the punishment for a fool.' Saladin's eyes betrayed his interest. 'And which of us here is the most foolish?' she added.

The words hung in the room in the silence that followed, all heads turning towards El Akir. For one, frightening moment, he really believed that the punishment he had so vividly described would fall on himself. He started back, fear written plainly all over him. Saladin turned away contemptuously and sat on the low seat, exchanging an eloquent look with his brother.

'El Akir,' he said, 'I can devise my own pleasures. Go with Sir William and let me hear you have treated him as an honoured guest. Let him take all liberties,' and he smiled in a friendly way at the Knight, 'except of course, liberty itself.' He waved a hand and the two men left the room silently. Saladin beckoned Barbara to come nearer.

'Are you afraid of me?'

Barbara shook her head and Saladin turned to his brother in mock surprise.

'If I cannot make women tremble, what hope have we to win this war?'

Barbara said, 'I know of no person who doesn't hold you in respect. There is a most healthy regard for your generalship, My Lord. I am not a man, so perhaps I don't fully understand what wars are all about, but I feel men of character do not care to fight against cowards.'

'There's philosophy here,' murmured Saladin.

'And wit, brother,' added Saphadin.

'Indeed. Now tell me the truth,' said the Sultan. 'You are not of these lands, yet you appear to be a stranger to Sir William.'

'I am . . . a traveller. I was with three friends. We arrived in the wood.'

'You rode into the wood?'

'No.'

'You walked into it,' hazarded Saphadin. Barbara shook

her head, wondering how she could explain enough without asking too much of their credulity.

'We arrived. In a box.'

'Ah! You were carried into the wood.'

Barbara felt it wise to agree with Saphadin on this point. Saladin sat back, rubbing a hand on his chin.

'A reluctant story-teller!'

'I could tell you . . . that I came from another world. Ruled by insects. Or that my friends and I recently visited Nero's Rome. Before that, that we were in an England far into the future.'

Saladin nodded slowly.

'I understand. You and your friends are a band of players? Entertainers? You are the story-teller?'

Barbara merely inclined her head, thankful to have found a way to justify her existence, without entering into a long and involved pattern of lies.

'Frankly, I tell you,' said the Sultan, 'you are an encumbrance. I do not dispense life and death lightly but you have no place in my military headquarters. A wise man would rid himself of you quickly and cleanly, and have done with it. So either you must serve a purpose here, or you have no purpose. We need diversion here and you shall provide it. If you succeed, you shall receive every kindness and comfort possible, and come to no harm. You shall grace my table tonight, with clothes more suitable to your new station.'

Barbara looked a little troubled, not quite understanding what Saladin meant.

'You are a self-confessed story-teller,' he said. 'If your stories beguile me, all will be well.'

Barbara said, 'Like Scheherazade?'

Saladin leant forward, a grim smile on his lips.

'Over whose head, you will recall, hung the sentence of death!'

CHAPTER FOUR

The Wheel of Fortune

As El Akir waited in the courtyard of Saladin's headquarters at Ramlah, cursing for allowing himself to be made a fool of by his prisoners, a tall, richly-dressed merchant sat drinking at a table. El Akir had noticed him as he strode out of the palace, dismissing him as one of a dozen foreign merchants who sought to make profit from the war.

It is always hard to understand a man without saving graces. All human beings have facets which make them admired, as much as those they may possess which dismay or repel. Those who knew El Akir found nothing to recommend him, for they recognized in him a man saturated with guilt, so much so that his life could only continue by laying extra evils, one above another, as if the man were tortured by the foul deeds he had committed and had to hide them by inventing fresh crimes; and far worse ones at that; curtaining off yesterday's depredations with new villainies.

All these things Luigi Ferrigo recognized; if not the actual details, certainly enough to know the type of man, for he was an expert judge of a particular sort of human nature. Ferrigo's fault lay in his total inability to apply his judgement to all manner of men. Put him in the company of fools, cowards, villains or the greedy and he would find a way to make each one his cat's-paw. Introduce him into a gathering of talent, honesty and good endeavour and he would withdraw within himself, become unapproachable and remote. So, as each man instinctively chooses the path in life he thinks will take him quickest to whatever his desires may be, Ferrigo's way was shadowy and devious. Some said of him that he'd rather earn one gold piece by guile than a fortune by straightforward dealing, while others were convinced he was so filled with the lust for riches, he would rise to any height, or sink to any depths to make a profit.

A woman came out of the palace, keeping to the shadows of the arched walk surrounding the courtyard. Luigi Ferrigo sat back in his chair, giving every evidence of sleep, while El Akir, seeing the woman he had been waiting for, drew himself into a small alcove. As she passed by him, he stepped out and gripped her arm. She gave a little shriek of fear and would have fallen to her knees, if he hadn't held her upright, his fingers pressing into the flesh of her arm painfully, almost bringing tears to her eyes.

'Sheyrah,' he whispered fiercely, 'where is the foreign woman? Tell me and you shall be rewarded.'

The woman stared into his eyes, frightened at the depths of hatred she saw. He shook her arm impatiently and with his other hand produced a ring from the pouch at his belt, a heavy thing of silver, clasping a large and beautiful yellow stone.

'Take it! Tell me! You are attending her, I know you are – the Sultan ordered it.'

As if the mention of Saladin gave her courage, she pulled her arm away and stepped back, rubbing the place where his fingers had gripped her. El Akir licked his lips and tried a slightly different approach. He held up the ring, so that it caught the light, and spoke more gently.

'Bring the foreign woman to me, Sheyrah, and you shall have this.' He looked at her to see what effect he was having and then took a step forward towards her as she shook her head stubbornly.

'Then deserve my enmity!'

'My Lord is greater than you,' Sheyrah said defiantly. El Akir's hand holding the ring bunched into a fist and

61

raised slightly in the air. Sheyrah cowered back, expecting the blow, when suddenly Luigi Ferrigo appeared, fanning his face with his hand, as if he had decided to try the cooler pleasures of the shade of the archway. El Akir's hand dropped to his side and Sheyrah hurried past him, disappearing into another part of the palace.

'She was a fool not to take the ring,' said Luigi casually and El Akir, who was just turning away, stiffened and swung around. 'But perhaps you were asking too much for it.'

The two men sized each other up for a few seconds and the Genoese knew he had the measure of his opposite number.

'I have some wine on a table over there,' he stated pleasantly.

'Why should I drink with you?'

'Because I have something to ask of someone. If only I knew their price.'

El Akir found himself being led out of the shadows and across the courtyard, ushered into a chair and given a cup of wine. He took it with a bad grace and drank deeply, liking the gentle richness of the amber liquid, which held a stronger body than the rougher wines he usually drank. Ferrigo added some more wine to the cup generously.

'This is a wine of France, a sample of some stock I carry in my ship which rests today at Acre. If you like it, I have a skin of it to give you.'

'I'm not bought by you, merchant,' growled El Akir. The other shook his head in pained surprise.

'The servants here have told me something about you, El Akir. You are an Emir, rich and prosperous already, with an army of your own. You have, I hear, a fine palace in the town of Lydda, a short ride from here. You do not think I imagine I can buy a person such as you with a skin of wine.'

'You know a lot. Why have you asked questions about me? Who are you? What are you doing in Ramlah?'

The merchant listened to all the questions tolerantly, taking a small drink from his own goblet, his eyes never leaving the Emir's face.

'I have travelled a long way to speak with your Sultan; a rather weary journey. Neither Saladin nor his brother will receive me. As to who I am, well, I am a merchant, as you guessed, and my business is to buy and sell.'

'It's nothing to me,' said El Akir, shaking his head a little as the strong wine began to take effect. 'I'm leaving Ramlah.'

'Returning to your palace at Lydda?'

'Yes, if it's any of your affair!'

Perhaps what holds you here is my affair.'

The Emir stared truculently across the table and got to his feet, an oath forming on his lips at the confusing way the stranger was speaking to him. Yet something in the other's manner stopped him and made him resume his seat again. Ferrigo smiled without any sign of triumph.

'We both have reasons for being in Ramlah, El Akir,' he said softly, leaning across the table. 'Can we not help each other?'

'Tell me your reason first,' said the other cautiously.

'Profit. I wish to arrange a safe conduct for caravans of goods to and from the Sultan's headquarters, from Ramlah to Tyre and back again.'

'We are at war,' replied El Akir stupidly, shaking his head again to try and clear away the wine fumes.

'Conrad of Tyre has fallen out with the King of the English and is sending an emissary here to make peace with your Sultan. Every army needs supplies and luxuries, while someone can be on hand to buy the booty captured in battle.'

El Akir nodded, trying to look intelligent. A fly buzzed around his face and he made an ineffectual jab at it with his hand.

'What is my part in this?' he said at last.

'Arrange an audience with the Sultan or his brother. I cannot pass the men who surround them.' Luigi Ferrigo lifted his goblet of wine and stared at the rim of it intently. 'But how could I return such a favour?'

'There is a woman here, an English one, who has made me look a fool,' the Emir blurted out. 'I want to take her to my palace at Lydda. We'll see who the fool is and who the master there. Help me – and you shall see the Sultan.'

There was a silence for a few seconds as the merchant raised the goblet to his lips and drained it, wiping his mouth delicately afterwards with a piece of silk he kept at his belt. He stood up.

'Arrange my audience for late this evening. When it is dark, wait by the stables. I shall bring the woman to you.'

El Akir watched the merchant walk away into the palace, suddenly finding that his head was hanging heavily on his neck. His eyelids seemed to be having trouble staying open. The fly returned with others and buzzed around him but this time he found no energy to drive them away. He settled back in the chair with one thing uppermost in his befuddled brain; that chance had brought him a way to satisfy the hate and vengeance towards the slim, attractive girl, whose smile had been worse than a hundred daggers through his heart. And, in contentment, El Akir let sleep overtake him.

Barbara listened seriously as Sheyrah warned her she had made an enemy, repeating the events of the meeting with El Akir and his obvious determination to find Barbara and exact some vengeance on her. There was no fear that he would try and attack her, Sheyrah promised, provided she stayed well within the Palace.

'I hear that he is returning to his own palace in Lydda,' said Sheyrah, as she combed Barbara's hair, 'so he will soon be far away, and you will be out of danger. Your hair is very lovely, my lady,' she said, as if trying to change the conversation for her own benefit, as much as for Barbara's; for her fear of the Emir was considerable. Barbara smiled at her in the mirror, then looked doubtfully at the clothes she wore.

She loved the sun and thought nothing better, in her own time in the 1960s, of sunburning herself in a bikini on the nearest beach at every available opportunity. But the beach was one thing, whereas being attired for a social engagement with Saladin – in a brief, two-piece bathing costume affair, embroidered with beads, the only other addition being the transparent Turkish sleeves and trouser legs fastened at the wrists and ankles with slim bands of gold silk – wasn't the same at all. She frowned uncertainly as Sheyrah bent down and slipped a beautiful pair of pointed slippers on her, sitting back on the floor, clapping her hands with delight.

'Are you sure this is what I should wear, Sheyrah?' she said anxiously. The servant rose to her feet, clucking her mouth in self-annoyance.

'Of course you are right, lady,' she said, 'and I am the most stupid of women to forget.' She crossed the room, ferreted about among some other clothes on a chest underneath the window, then returned to Barbara triumphantly, bearing a small piece of diaphanous silk in her hands. She fastened the yashmak behind Barbara's head.

'Now,' she said proudly, 'see how you look! All men will stare at the beauty of your eyes this night.'

'But the rest of me,' said Barbara, in a small voice. She searched for some way to explain, conscious that in Sheyrah's eyes, the briefness of the costume mattered less than that the face was covered. 'Sheyrah,' she said suddenly, inspiration coming to her assistance, 'I'm not used to this climate. You wouldn't have me start shivering in front of the Sultan. He might think I was afraid of him. And besides, how am I supposed to tell him stories, when my teeth are chattering?'

Sheyrah shook her head, bothered by the problem.

'Could I not wear the cloak Sir William bought for me?'

'You may wear a cloak,' replied Sheyrah, 'but it must be of better quality. I will search and find one.' Sheyrah bustled out of the room through a bead curtain and began to delve into another chest, in the ante-chamber beyond.

Barbara turned her mind to the role she was going to have to play for the Sultan. At first, the idea of relating a story to an audience had terrified her to death, until she had realized that worrying about it was simply making it worse. Then she had remembered the rich heritage of the English literary world, and so many plots and ideas had filled her brain that she hadn't known which to choose and which to abandon. Now she sat quietly, composing her thoughts, selecting what she felt might divert and entertain Saladin. Shakespeare, of course, was the very first on the list. 'Hamlet' she considered too difficult to put across; 'Romeo and Juliet', however, seemed an excellent blend of drama and romance. She felt, also that she could slightly change

'The Merchant of Venice', making Shylock a Syrian or an Arab to bring the story closer to Saladin's understanding and provide him with a character with whom he could sympathize. As she pictured herself actually relating any of these stories under the unwavering gaze of what she knew would be a most critical audience, a cold, clammy hand of fear closed around her heart, but she resolutely pushed that vision from her mind and started to tabulate a list of authors in her mind.

Suddenly she saw a hand appear in the archway leading to the corridor beyond, and a tall, richly-dressed man slipped into the room, a finger to his lips, his eyes burning with intensity.

'I am Luigi Ferrigo,' he whispered urgently, 'and I have come to set you free.' He stared about the room and spotted the figure of the servant in the ante-room, sorting through the clothes.

'Who sent you?' asked Barbara, a wild hope surging through her, mostly that she would be released from the role of story-teller she was inwardly dreading so much. 'Was it Sir William?'

Ferrigo nodded quickly. In his right hand, he held a pair of gloves; on the back of each was embroidered a snake picked out with a series of small pearls. He laid them down on the table, gesturing urgently with both his hands to lend force to his persuasion.

'I have a horse for you in the stable, and a guide to take you to Jaffa. But you must come at once!'

Barbara nodded and got silently to her feet, then thought of the flimsiness of her costume.

'I'll need a covering of some kind,' she pleaded. The Genoese pursed his lips then swung the heavy dark cloak from his own shoulders and wrapped it around her.

'Come!' He snatched up his gloves, urging her through the archway, with a last look back at the servant to make sure she was still occupied. Hastily but without any signs of panic, he conducted her through a series of corridors, keeping as much to the shadows where possible, stopping sometimes and listening; his head bent forward as he searched with acute hearing to find if danger lay around a corner. Once they slipped past a Saracen guard, who stood half asleep, leaning on a lance – and just before they reached the head of a small stone stairway which, the man whispered to Barbara, led down to the stables. They had to negotiate themselves past an open doorway of a well-lit room, from within the depths of which they could both distinguish the sounds of several men talking. The merchant risked a look in and, satisfied that the men were heavily engaged in a game of chance, hurried Barbara across and down the flight of stairs.

Breathing rather heavily, he held her back with one arm as he peered out of the archway which led out to a small street, on the other side of which was a half-open door leading to the stables. He glanced anxiously up at the moon, which rode high in the cloudless sky.

'Stay here,' he breathed, 'and run across to that door when I call.' Barbara nodded, and he stepped out boldly, turning his head quickly from right to left. She watched him walk across to the little door, push it open and then look back at her. Even before he could open his mouth, she clutched the cloak around her tightly and ran across to join him. He closed the door behind her, took her by the arm, gently but firmly, and led her to the other end of the stables. The horses tethered in their stalls stared at the hurrying couple as they went by, the pride of the Grand Sultan's collection, each one as black as pitch, with coats that rippled and gleamed in the moonlight filtering through the small windows high up on the side walls.

'Your guide should be at the other end of the stables,' whispered Ferrigo, 'the horses ready for immediate departure.'

'How can I ever thank you,' said Barbara gratefully.

Ferrigo smiled at her, and it was at that moment that a tiny icicle of suspicion formed at the back of her neck, sending little droplets of shivers down her spine. She heard the sound of footfalls behind her, watched the smile grow on Ferrigo's lips, the eyes narrowing with expectancy, watched almost with fascination as his tongue appeared and ran over his top lip. Her heart started to beat faster, certain now that she had been betrayed in some way, and she took a step to one side. A hand gripped hold of her arm and twisted it behind her cruelly and the face of El Akir was thrust into hers, the livid scar suddenly picked out by a shaft of moonlight, heightening it and making it a symbol of terror.

In a few seconds, the Emir had tied a piece of cloth tightly around her mouth, while Ferrigo bound her hands in front of her with a piece of rope El Akir produced from his belt. She made no attempt to struggle but just stood listlessly, while the two men made her helpless, the heavy weight of despair robbing her of any resistance, any thoughts of escape. El Akir led her to where two horses had been brought just inside the stable doors.

'You have settled my terms?' inquired Luigi Ferrigo sharply. El Akir lifted Barbara up on to her horse, and then mounted his own, holding both reins in his left hand. He lent across, slipped a rope through those securing Barbara's hands and looped the other end around his right wrist.

'I have arranged your audience with the Sultan and his brother. You are to dine with them tonight.'

Barbara turned her head and stared down at the merchant contemptuously, wondering how he could hand over the body and soul of a human being for such a trivial reason.

As if he read her thoughts, Luigi Ferrigo turned away as the Emir urged the horses to a gallop so swiftly that the impetus had Barbara grabbing desperately for the long mane of her steed.

Luigi Ferrigo staggered backwards as the horses shot

away, a cloud of dust spraying up and covering part of his robe. With a muttered curse, he reached for the gloves at his belt, intending to brush himself. He stared at the single glove in his hand, wondering where its fellow was. He started to go back on his tracks, his eyes bent on the ground, searching out every dark corner.

The two horses galloped away from the Palace through the town of Ramlah, startling the few people who were in the streets and making them step into doorways and press themselves against the walls. One look at the hard, set face of the Emir, bent forward low over his mount, urging every inch of speed out of it, was enough to make them turn their faces away and close their minds to questions, although some of them wondered who the beautiful girl could be whose hair streamed out behind her.

The horses sped out of the town and into the surrounding country, across fields baked hard in the long summer, every yard adding to El Akir's triumph, every inch increasing Barbara's desperation and despair.

Luigi Ferrigo had failed to find his glove and would have put the affair out of his mind as a trifling matter, except that somehow it irritated him. He was a careful man and the gloves had been specially designed for him, and had been very costly. More than this, he had covered every inch of the ground he had walked, except, of course, for that part of the Palace he and Barbara had covered so secretly. The merchant had no intention of venturing back there again, merely to find a piece of wearing apparel. Finally, back in his room, bored with the problem of the missing article, he made a complete change of clothes to be ready for his audience with Saladin and tossed the single useless glove on to a window ledge. He stared out of the window, trying to forget the expression in the beautiful girl's eyes as she looked down at him from the horse. Then a servant entered and announced he had come to conduct him to the Great Sultan.

All thoughts of the events of the earlier part of the evening now fell away from him as he planned his approach, discarding this idea, adopting another. The servant conducted him to a wide archway guarded by two magnificently tall fighting warriors of the Sultan's own race, the Kurds, and into a large, pleasant chamber festooned with draperies and hangings, furnished with low couches and cushions and luxuriant carpets.

Saladin sat on one of the couches, his brother Saphadin standing beside him, and both the men received their visitor with smiles and words of friendship, the Sultan gesturing to the merchant to sit beside him. Saphadin tapped his hands together lightly and servants carried in a long, low table upon which were some goblets and a wine-jug, dishes of sweetmeats and fruit. Ferrigo was most interested in the wine jug, which he guessed was of Roman origin, probably as early as 50 B.C. He questioned Saladin about it and the Sultan complimented him on his knowledge.

'This is an actual reminder of Gaius Julius Caesar, and his stay in Egypt. It is one of a collection presented by the General to Cleopatra, the Queen of Egypt, and made specially for the occasion.'

A servant poured some wine from the wine-jug under discussion and handed the goblet to Ferrigo.

'Now tell me,' said the Sultan when they had tasted the wine, 'what is your business here at Ramlah?'

'I would have you imagine Europe as a great shop, Your Highness, constantly full of customers begging for perfumes and cloth, ivory and gold and spices. All these things have been scarce of late.'

'Because of the war,' pointed out Saphadin.

'And wars are costly,' replied Ferrigo. 'The sale of these items would produce a vast profit.'

Saladin nodded thoughtfully. 'As you say, wars are costly. And we are not averse to trade, merchant, nor do we turn

71

away from profit. But our enemies hold the coast from Acre to Jaffa. You cannot imagine you would make the land journey, for you would be a prey to marauders and thieves every step of the way.'

'No, I have ships, Your Highness. And my information is that Conrad of Tyre wishes to make peace with you.'

The brothers exchanged glances.

'You are well informed,' murmured Saphadin, 'although we have not concluded any terms with Conrad.'

'What you are seeking,' said Saladin directly, 'is a concession. Is that not so?'

The merchant inclined his head. 'With safe conduct guaranteed for caravans to and from the town of Tyre.'

'And where is our profit in this merchant adventuring? When the goods are sold in Genoa?'

'No, My Lord. In my ships at Tyre, I have stocks of leather harnesses and bridles for your horses, a quantity of swords and a thousand daggers of exquisite workmanship. I also have cattle and sheep. What I am suggesting is that these goods go against the goods I am to receive from you, or from your allies through your patronage and introduction.'

Saladin thought for a moment and then rose to his feet. Ferrigo stood up at the same time, out of politeness, wondering if the interview was at an end.

'I like your proposition, merchant,' remarked the Sultan, 'but I would know more about you first. Now a matter has occurred here in my court which you shall help me judge. In this way, I shall see the truth of your mind and the quality of your heart.'

Ferrigo bowed, convinced that he was very near success. Saphadin moved to the archway, as the servant who had conducted Ferrigo to the Sultan's chamber appeared. Something was passed between them, and as Saphadin returned, Ferrigo saw him tucking some dark object into the sleeve of his flowing robes. Then his attention was diverted as Sheyrah was led through the archway by a guardsman. She threw herself down full length in front of Saladin, who bent his head near the merchant.

'This is purely a domestic matter, but since it concerns a person who is more of your way of life than ours, your advice will be welcome.'

Ferrigo bowed, rather complimented at the way the evening was progressing. The woman on the floor began to moan pitifully, begging her master not to blame her. Saphadin ordered her to be silent, in words that brooked no denial. The woman bit her lips and now kneeled on the floor, bending her head down so that it touched the carpet.

'A prisoner has escaped,' said Saladin casually, 'a woman I had hoped would divert my court. I had reason to believe she was a story-teller.'

Ferrigo suppressed the smile that itched at the corners of his mouth. This was ironic indeed. Then he looked towards the arch as another guard conducted in a tall, dark-haired young man, dressed in clothes that Ferrigo recognized as English.

'Now we are all gathered,' said Saladin. He reached down and raised the woman up slightly. 'Tell me your name.'

'Sheyrah,' she stammered, half in a whisper.

'Then listen to me well, Sheyrah! I shall not punish you if you tell me the truth. Where is the English lady you were serving?'

'I do not know, Your Eminence, I swear I do not! She begged me to fetch her a cloak to wear, complaining of the cold. I went to search one out, and when I returned there was no sign of her.'

'And that is all you know?'

'I swear it! I swear it!'

'Very well.' Saladin looked across at the man in English clothes, turned his head to Ferrigo and whispered who he was. Ferrigo nodded.

'Now, Sir William, do you know nothing of this affair?'

'I do not, Great Sultan,' replied the knight firmly. 'I would not encourage a lady to venture out alone.'

'I believe you. Nor do I believe she would go by herself.' He looked at Ferrigo. 'What is your opinion?'

'This lady of whom you speak must have had a companion, an accomplice who helped her escape.' He was glad to see the gleam of approval in the Sultan's eyes.

'Yes, that is indeed possible.'

'But improbable,' broke in Sir William. 'She had no gold pieces, or coin of any kind. Neither did she have any jewellery. This woman will tell you that I had to buy her a cloak to cover her.' Sheyrah nodded in confirmation. 'So you see, she had no way to bribe any of your people to aid her escape,' continued the Knight. 'I cannot believe that in the short time she was here she made such firm friendships that they would break their loyalty to you, Sultan, and help her.'

'I like the way you reason,' murmured Saladin. 'Let us establish the facts we know of this mystery. The prisoner could not escape by herself, could not bribe her way to freedom.' He turned to the Genoese merchant again, as if for his opinion.

'I confess myself defeated,' said Ferrigo, assuming a frown of concentration.

'Come, merchant, come! Is there not another reason to explain this woman's sudden disappearance?'

Ferrigo rested one arm upon another, his left hand to his chin, apparently deep in thought. Finally he shook his head.

'No, Your Highness, I cannot unravel this problem.'

Sir William said, 'She was abducted,' and Saladin nodded.

'Yes, Sir William, your mind is sharp. It was not a friend she had made in my court, but an enemy.'

'El Akir!'

'The same. But he was not alone. He could not tempt her from the safety of her room. Someone else must have led her to the Emir.' He looked down at Sheyrah thoughtfully, and she shook her head vehemently.

'It was not me,' she wailed, tears rolling down her face, 'I warned her of the Emir, El Akir. I liked the foreign lady . . .'

Saladin held up his hand and stemmed the flow of words. 'I believe you, Sheyrah. Tell us what you discovered in the room, after the prisoner had vanished.'

Luigi Ferrigo watched, with a horrid fascination, as Sheyrah produced a glove from the folds of her garments. As if in slow motion, Saladin reached out a hand and took it from the woman on her knees and held it up in front of his eyes. Suddenly his eyes darted towards the merchant, and they were as cold and hard as black pebbles on a beach.

'Is this your glove?' he asked in a merciless voice. The question seemed to hang in the room, and every face was turned towards the merchant. A nerve began to beat in his throat and he felt the sweat start out on his forehead.

'No. No, it is not. Of course it is not,' he stammered, incapable of seeing a way out of the trap the Sultan had laid for him. Dimly he saw Saphadin produce another glove and hand it to his brother, who placed the two together and matched them as a pair.

'Then why did we find the one that pairs with it in your room?'

Sir William took three steps across to Ferrigo, shot out his hands and gripped him around the throat, forcing him to his knees.

'You vile, treacherous dog! Where is she?'

He shook the hapless man violently, and then threw him down to the ground in disgust.

Saladin said, 'We know where your friend has been taken.' Sir William swung round and faced the Sultan, the question trembling on his lips.

'El Akir has gone, and so have two horses from the stables. Questions will be asked in the town, but I have no doubt

75

that the Emir has abducted her and taken her to his palace at Lydda.'

'Will you send after her and demand that she be returned?'

Sir William stared at Saladin as he shook his head.

'But why? Why not?'

'Because she is just one woman, Sir William. El Akir, for all his villainies, is an ally. He commands an army upon which I may have to rely in time of battle. I cannot quarrel with him until his use to me is over.'

Sir William immediately started to plead with the Sultan to reconsider and Luigi Ferrigo, seeing that they were occupied, and realizing it might be his one last chance, suddenly sprang to his feet and ran towards the archway.

What vain hopes he had of rushing past the guards he knew would be outside the chamber, making his way to the stables, stealing a horse and fleeing from danger: no one can estimate. Desperation born of fear forced him to act without proper thought. A single, unhurried shout by Saphadin brought one of the guards into view in the archway, his curved sword ready for command. Saphadin brought his hand down sharply, just as the merchant tried to slip past the guard, and with a swift circular motion the sword flashed through the air and struck down at Ferrigo, cutting deeply into the base of his neck. With a scream of pain, he fell out of sight of the watching men, around the corner of the archway. The guard took one short step and the sword was raised again. There was a piteous cry for mercy and then a half strangulated gurgle as retribution struck again, ending the life of a man who had lived by treachery and deceit.

The death of Luigi Ferrigo brought little satisfaction to Sir William in the long hours that followed. Other matters concerned the Sultan and his brother, Saphadin; there were incredible rumours that King Richard had offered his sister Joanna in marriage to Saphadin to bring the war to a speedy conclusion and achieve with peace what a trial of arms had failed to win, so the Knight was left to his own devices. His life was not unpleasant, for such was Saladin's chivalry that it was natural for him to command that Sir William was well treated. Daily exercise was permitted, food and all manner of delicacies were provided and the rooms set aside for his use in the Palace were well furnished and comfortable – but shadows appeared under his eyes and his face became thin and strained, sleep was difficult and relaxation impossible, for the Knight constantly tortured himself with a thousand horrific fears for Barbara in the hands of the vicious enemy who had seized and carried her off. Somehow he couldn't rid himself of the thought that if only he hadn't agreed to let her aid him in his pretence of being King Richard, all her troubles might have been avoided. Daily he sought such company as he was allowed, men-at-arms and servants, the philosophers and learned men whom Saladin loved to group around him at his court; anyone, in fact, who was prepared to sit with him and answer his questions about El Akir. A terrible picture emerged, which did nothing to bring him peace of mind, for no one offered any consolation for the abducted girl, and nowhere could he find a person who could say that the Emir had a spark of mercy or a saving grace in his character, or remember one single act of human kindness he had ever done.

And then Sir William was told by his personal servant that a representative of King Richard had arrived at Ranlah, under personal truce, to seek the release of two prisoners. Sir William requested he be allowed to talk to the new arrival and soon a guard ushered in a young, well-bronzed figure who wore the white surcoat emblazoned with the cross so proudly.

'I am Sir Ian, of Jaffa,' announced the new arrival, 'sent by the King to arrange your release, in company with the lady who was captured with you.' Ian saw how the other man's shoulders sagged listlessly, and a feeling of uneasiness crept over him.

'She is here, Sir William, surely?'

'She was here,' replied the other, and related what had happened, until all the buoyant hopes that had helped Ian on his journey from Jaffa to Ramlah, began to sink in the depths of despondency as the grim story was unfolded. The two men stared out of the window, each fully occupied with his thoughts. Finally, Ian turned away.

'Of course, I shall go to Lydda and search for her.'

'Will Saladin permit you to do that? Wander freely within his territory?'

'He cannot prevent it. I am here under personal truce, an emissary of King Richard. I must find her, Sir William, and take her back to Jaffa.'

Ian looked keenly at the Knight, trying to read the expression on his face. Eventually, their eyes met.

'I hope you will find a way to settle the matter with El Akir, at least.'

'What are you afraid of? Tell me about the man.'

'I could talk to you about him from now until the sun rises again. He is a black-hearted villain, the worst kind of man alive.' He sat down hopelessly on a small stool and leaned his arms on his knees, a tiredness creeping into his voice, as if he were putting into words, for the first time, thoughts that had haunted him for too long.

'El Akir is one whose pleasures are inhuman. He will not spare his victims any humiliation his agile brain can well devise. He is a past master in the arts of torture, not simply of the flesh, but of the mind and soul as well. He does not kill lightly, because he prefers to prolong suffering, pain and mental anguish. Search into the darkest corners of your imagination, invent the worst misdeeds you can, and still El Akir will surpass them by a hundred-fold. All you can do, Ian, is pray that death has brought a merciful release; for there'll be no hope for her alive.'

At this very moment, El Akir led Barbara's horse over the brow of a hill and brought both the animals to a halt, staring down at the town of Lydda beneath them. Barbara had been given no food or water during the journey and the sun was so heavy on her unprotected head that she felt as if a steel band had been fixed tightly just above her eyebrows. The whole of her body felt weary with the enforced ride and the cords around her wrists had bitten deeply into the flesh, making the hands numb as the flow of blood had been stopped. She felt the Emir's eyes on her and she lifted her head wearily, determined to hide as much of her suffering from him as she could. He pointed forward towards the town with one hand, pulling cruelly on the rope attached to her with the other. She bit her lip as a stab of pain cut into her wrists and he grinned slightly.

'There is Lydda. My army is encamped around it. A new

life is about to unfold for you.' He leaned towards her, a glitter of satisfaction mirrored all over his face. 'There will be difficult lessons to learn and hard rules to follow. You will know sorrow and shame, sleep will be driven away by tears. You will hope to kill yourself, or try to make me kill you. But death will be far in the distant future, only to be given when all your colours have faded, your spirit is crushed and your mind has nearly gone.'

He spurred his horse with his heels suddenly with a shout of evil joy, nearly pulling Barbara off her mount, and the two horses galloped down the hill towards Lydda.

CHAPTER FIVE

The Doctor in Disgrace

One might have imagined that the Doctor and his ward, Vicki, would be having a reasonably pleasant time in King Richard's Palace at Jaffa, and so it was for a short time after Ian rode out with his small escort towards the direction of the Sultan's headquarters at Ramlah. Richard liked richness around him, and rarely took his pleasures singly. About him were gathered all the men of wit and good conversation available and the Chamberlain saw that a steady supply of entertainers provided as many different forms of entertainment as existed, all for the diversion of the court. Meats and vegetables, fruits and nuts, wines and delicacies of every conceivable kind poured out of the visiting ships in the little harbour to grace the tables of the King.

For, uneasy and of no fixed duration though it might be, peace was on hand. The armies licked their wounds and rested their tired muscles, turning their minds to their homes and families, their businesses, trades and crafts.

The Chamberlain was the busiest man by far. Administrator of the King's court, he was tall, with an imposing manner, and could deliver a look so cold and haughty that even the wilfully disobedient shuddered in awe and tried to mend their ways. Rising with the sun each day, he interviewed his various lieutenants and dealt with the problems they brought to him quickly and precisely. A system of runners was always in operation between himself and wherever the King happened to be in the Palace, so that he could leave what he was doing at any moment and deal immediately with any request or order Richard might require he supervise.

As one might guess, he possessed a phenomenal memory. Frequently, he was called upon to produce a certain entertainer who had pleased Richard or Joanna, or one of the nobles at the court; one who had not performed for some days. Instantly, the Chamberlain delved into the recesses of his mind, either knowing where such a person was to be found or who would know. By far the greatest feat of memory he could claim was the record of the wardrobe of the Palace, for he was often asked to provide clothes for visitors whose entire possessions had been stolen, quite apart from maintaining the standard of dress necessary to the servants of the King. Thus, he always kept a good supply of clothes of all descriptions ready for any emergency and because he was the keeper of the Household Purse, he watched each and every article with care and devotion.

He was certain that the clothes worn by the three new friends of the King were from his own wardrobe. He was not the sort of man who made mistakes but neither was he unfair enough to accuse without absolute proof. He descended to the rooms where the clothes were kept and made a diligent search, eventually satisfying himself that the clothes worn by the Doctor, Ian and Vicki (although he thought of her, of course, as a page-boy) were indeed identical to those now missing from his collection. But, again, he decided against facing them with an accusation before he had investigated the matter properly. His search of the wardrobe revealed other articles to be missing and his alert mind began to put a simple two to a simpler two: a thief with light fingers – a sale and a profit. Thus he undertook a tour of all the clothing shops in Jaffa.

Jaffa was not so large, nor the Chamberlain so faint-hearted that such an unenviable task should worry him.

The Chamberlain covered every stall of every shop in every street, inevitably coming upon Ben Daheer's establishment.

Almost immediately, he spotted a pile of clothes of English design and let his hands wander over them idly as he talked to the shopkeeper, satisfying himself that they were, indeed, the property of the Palace.

By the force of his considerable personality, the Chamberlain persuaded Ben Daheer to accompany him, pretending that he could arrange for the shopkeeper's talent for making clothes to be brought to the King's attention. It took no urging for Ben Daheer to order his eldest son to watch his establishment while he clutched some samples of cloth under his arm and hurried to keep up with his new benefactor. The Chamberlain led him into the Palace, through several corridors, finally stopping in front of a heavy door. He knocked upon it, while the man beside him straightened his clothes and wiped the perspiration from his face, thinking he was being taken directly to the King. He was nervous and glad of the Chamberlain's hand on his arm. A servant opened the door.

The Doctor, who was enjoying a meal with Vicki, looked up with a faint air of annoyance at being disturbed. He heard the Chamberlain order the servant from the room, watched him close the door himself and lean against it. Ben Daheer bowed nervously, realizing he wasn't in the presence of Royalty and wondering where he had met the white-haired man before.

'What is the meaning of this intrusion?' asked the Doctor. The Chamberlain advanced into the room, bringing Ben Daheer with him.

'Have you ever seen this man before?'

'Yes, I was trying to remember when,' replied the shopkeeper.

'He came to your shop?'

'Yes. Ah, yes, now I remember. He searched among my cloth but found nothing that suited him.'

The Doctor's eyes narrowed and he regarded the
Chamberlain carefully. It was quite clear where the man
was aiming, but the Doctor kept his peace for the moment
and signalled to Vicki to keep well in the background,
although he could see she was bursting with questions.

'Did you miss any of your possessions after this man had
visited you?'

'Why, yes. Some clothes had gone.' Ben Daheer glanced
about him nervously, remembering that the things he had
missed had been stolen clothes he had acquired from
Thatcher, the Palace servant. 'Just a few miserable garments, Your Eminence,' he said indifferently. The Chamberlain walked across to the Doctor, plucked at the sleeve
nearest to him and held it out.

'Clothes like this?'

The Doctor pulled his arm away sharply and stood up so
rapidly that his chair crashed backwards to the floor.

'This is quite insufferable!' he raged. 'How dare you burst in here with these insulting accusations.'

'Clothes like these were stolen from the Palace. . . .'

'But how,' interrupted the Doctor, 'do you know these are the same? I mean exactly. They may *resemble* yours.'

'I am quite certain the clothes you are wearing belong to the Palace wardrobe. We keep a large supply here, for travellers may not be able to transport wearing apparel. It is my duty to see those who have audience with the King are properly attired.'

'So you carry a large stock of clothes, do you? How large? How many items?'

'That is beside the point,' replied the Chamberlain angrily. The Doctor darted out a finger, pointing it straight into the Chamberlain's face.

'It is *just* the point, my friend. You have in your Palace wardrobe shoes, buckles, stockings, cloaks, belts, hats, caps, coats, tunics, leggings, vestments, capes – all in different colours, sizes and designs. You dare to stand here and tell me you're *certain* these garments belong to you!'

The Chamberlain nodded but the Doctor had seen the momentary indecision on his face and followed up his advantage.

'Where is the mark on these clothes proving they are yours?' he said sharply. 'Where is your bill of sale?'

The Chamberlain opened his mouth to reply, then closed it again, realizing he was on unsure ground. The Doctor's manner softened suddenly. He was an eminently fair man and knew perfectly well he was in the wrong, even if the present difficulties had been brought about by Barbara's abduction.

'I will tell you what happened,' murmured the Doctor, ushering the Chamberlain to a chair. 'My . . . page and I met a rough fellow in Jaffa from whom we bought these simple garments. Our own clothes were in a terrible state. Now whether this uncouth man had stolen the clothes from you first is another matter. Have you been missing things from the wardrobe?'

'Yes, without a doubt,' agreed the Chamberlain.

'Then someone in your service at the Palace is a pilferer. Someone who has access to the wardrobe. Of course, if you are certain these clothes I am wearing belong to you, I shall see they are returned to you immediately.'

Vicki breathed an inward sigh of relief as the Chamberlain's manner became much warmer, mentally blessing the Doctor for wriggling out of the awkward situation.

'Of course, my page and I have no clothes here,' the Doctor went on, 'and also, it seems to me, this honest merchant has been involved without much proper cause. Or profit.'

Ben Daheer, who had been following the conversation with increasing nervousness, terrified he would be revealed as a buyer of stolen goods, perked up his head at the sound of the word profit and his face brightened visibly.

'Since we need clothes,' the Doctor continued persuasively, 'couldn't we employ the merchant to make us outfits?'

The Chamberlain, also conscious he had brought Ben Daheer to the Palace on a false pretext, immediately agreed. The Doctor smiled.

'And what do you think he should be paid?' he asked pleasantly. The Chamberlain rubbed his chin reflectively.

'Well, well,' said the Doctor, before he could reply, 'I'll leave it to you. You pay him whatever you think.'

The Chamberlain stared at the Doctor.

'I? Pay the merchant?'

'You are the Keeper of the Household Purse, are you not?'

Once again, the Doctor produced a battery of argument to support his plan, and eventually the Chamberlain held up his hands wearily then drew out a pouch from his belt. The Doctor took it from his hand, extracted six gold pieces from it and handed them to Ben Daheer, returning the half-empty purse to the defeated Chamberlain. Ben Daheer rubbed his hands over the coins in glee and was just about to launch into a long speech of gratitude when the Doctor cut him short.

'Let us not say anything more until you have cut and stitched our clothes. There! This tiresome business has come to a happy conclusion for all of us.'

He turned and grinned at the Chamberlain's long face.

'I know, I know. You think that six gold pieces are too much for a single outfit each for my page and myself. But be contented, my dear sir. A man in my position needs all kinds of things to wear. I shall see your six gold pieces are used in the proper way. Besides costumes for our immediate use, this honest fellow and I will see that I am dressed for any occasion.'

'My Lord, it is obvious to me that you are extremely important,' said Ben Daheer, 'but to do you justice I might well exceed the six gold pieces you have generously showered on me.'

The Doctor waved a hand grandly and Vicki turned away to hide her smile.

'Whatever the sum is, my good man,' he said airily, 'the Chamberlain will meet it.'

Before the Chamberlain could argue, servants in the corridors started up a cry of his name. A servant knocked at the door and hurried in. Ben Daheer turned and then gasped in surprise.

'It was him! He is your thief. His name is Thatcher.'

Thatcher, the culprit, gave a shout of terror as the Chamberlain ran after him. The Doctor put his arm around the shopkeeper's shoulders.

'Well, well. Now that we have that little matter settled, let us discuss the clothes you shall make for my page and myself.'

None of them saw the Princess Joanna walk past the door, hesitate for a second and then stand in the doorway.

'You will make us some fine clothes, my friend,' the Doctor was saying. Vicki made a face.

'Must I go on pretending to be a page, Doctor? Can't I be a girl again? The dresses are so attractive.'

'A pretty deception,' murmured the Princess.

In the silence that followed she walked nearer to them, as all three bowed, looking at the Doctor seriously.

'Why have you deceived us all?'

'Your Highness, this is a dangerous land, and my ward is as young as I am old. I beg of you to remember that of the four in our party only one was young and virile and capable of any trial of strength. It is, I confess, a trick – but one intended for the protection of a young and innocent person, not to gain profit or favour.'

The Doctor bowed as he completed his speech and Joanna smiled at him, half in admiration and half in reproof.

'You are a good advocate, sir, and I shall not persist in this matter. But see that the merchant here dresses your ward in more of a feminine fashion. Her style of clothes,' she added ironically, 'might upset the even tenor of our way of life if it became known the boy was a girl. Legs as slim and straight were meant to be covered, not emphasized.'

Vicki restrained any ideas that sprang into her head of describing other fashions which occurred to her, in times long after the Princess lived. She simply kissed the hand that Joanna held out in affection, glad to be rid of a costume she detested.

'Go with this trader,' said Joanna gently, 'and see that he designs good fashions for you. You shall be company for me, sing and learn to play an instrument.'

Joanna watched Vicki and Ben Daheer as they bowed and left the room, then she moved to a chair and sat down. The Doctor gestured to some wine and a platter of fruit, and when she refused asked if she would object if he poured himself some of the wine.

'Please continue,' she said, 'and seat yourself, for I wish to talk to you.'

'I'm very grateful for your interest in my ward, Your Highness,' the Doctor said when he had sat down.

'I note your gratitude. I cannot ask you to repay me, but I have something to ask you. There's something new in you, yet something older than the sky itself. You give me confidence and I value knowing you, sensing I can trust you. Yet all the while I am aware that we have exchanged but a few brief words, and known each other for hardly any time at all.'

'Madam, your beauty alone earns my interest, if I may venture to say such a thing. Your mind commands my respect. Whatever I can do in your service, shall be done.'

Joanna smiled at the Doctor's gallantry and composed her thoughts.

'I am my brother's favourite,' she said, at length, 'yet now I find I am excluded from his confidence. Oh, he smiles at me and talks of this and that; he pays me compliments and seems to listen so intently when I talk, I might, for all the world, be Socrates returned to gift him with a wise advice. Here at Richard's court, I do not play at politics. All are Richard's men, heart and soul, so there is no one to whom I can honestly go, nor any who will come to me in confidence.'

'Are you sure you are not imagining this change of attitude?' asked the Doctor, rather disturbed at the position into which he was being drawn. Richard had already exacted a promise from Ian, Vicki and himself to keep his secret of the marriage plan between Saphadin and Joanna. And now his sister had guessed that something was going on behind her back.

'I sense Richard has made a plan of which I am a part,' she said slowly, examining the Doctor's face. He never moved a muscle, and met her gaze blankly.

'I can hardly ask the King,' he murmured.

'But if you learn anything, you will tell me?' She entreated him. The Doctor rose to his feet.

'Madam, if I hear of anything that is in my power to repeat to you, I shall do so, I promise you.'

'Then will you go to the King now? He is locked away with the Earl of Leicester, and again I sense that I am the subject of their conversation.'

'Madam, I cannot burst in on your brother's private councils,' objected the Doctor.

'But Richard wants you to be present. His messenger will arrive here to conduct you to his presence soon, for I heard him give the order. But when you have attended this meeting, will you come to me and tell me if my suspicions are correct, and what my brother's planning holds in store for me?'

The Doctor almost felt inclined to break Richard's confidence there and then, but he said nothing, sure that if he did he would regret it.

'Do I have your friendship?' she insisted, making a direct appeal.

'Unless the King binds me to secrecy, I shall come to you and tell you anything which might endanger or distress you.'

He could see that Joanna wanted to press him further and try to persuade him to go to even greater lengths for her, but at that moment there was a knock on the door and one of Richard's personal servants bowed and announced that he had come to conduct the Doctor to the King. Joanna remained seated, smiling sadly as the Doctor bent over her hand and kissed it, and he carried the vision of her face as he followed the servant through the corridors. Somehow or other, he told himself, he must wriggle out of the net of court intrigue which seemed to be enmeshing him. His place at the court of King Richard, and Vicki's, was tenuous enough already, without adding fresh difficulties. But he could see no way out for the present, and just had to hope that either Richard would make his plans public or that Joanna wouldn't press him too much.

He was ushered into Richard's council chamber, where the King waved him into the room. The Earl of Leicester stood listening as the King moved about the room talking.

'. . . and when Sir Ian is with us again,' he was saying rather loudly, 'he'll bring back William des Preaux and the answer to my several letters. News, my Lord of Leicester! And I have great hopes that it will favour us.'

The Doctor knew instinctively why he had been invited to attend this meeting between the King and his staunchest fighting leader. Richard was nervous. A fighter himself, rather than a politician, he had stepped into a world he did not understand, where pacts and clauses, bargains and words were the weapons, and he was already finding his new role a difficult one. To a man of action, the concentration of forces, manœuvres on the field of battle and disposition of mounted men and archers were necessary arts. What mattered most was that there would have to be a distinct end in view – the conflict of arms, and the fight would either be lost or won. Richard knew the value of reserves, the art of thrust and parry, a violent charge of mounted horse or a deliberate feint before a major blow. But in council or political strategy he was unhappily ill at ease and the Doctor could sense at once that even the simple task of explaining his plans to the Earl of Leicester was no easy matter. So Richard had brought in the Doctor to support him, the one objective person in all his court.

'Tell me what you have in mind, Sire,' Leicester said eagerly, his left hand gripping the hilt of his sword. 'A new demand of Saladin? A new victory like Arsuf?'

Richard looked across at the Doctor who could plainly see something of the trepidation in his eyes.

'Not this time, Leicester. I have had another thought.'

He began to walk again, as if it gave him confidence, one

hand tucked into the ornamental belt around his waist, the other rubbing the back of his neck. Finally, he made up his mind to escape the issue no longer, folded his arms and faced the puzzled Earl of Leicester.

'I am going to give my sister's hand in marriage to Saladin's brother, Saphadin. It will make an end of this war, yet achieve our purpose all in one.'

The Earl stared back unbelievingly, the veins knotting in his throat, his chin hardening as he clamped his lips together. The Doctor moved forward slowly, feeling that he must support the King, and justify the reason for his presence.

'An admirable scheme, Sire, and one deserving success.'

Richard looked at him gratefully. The Earl's head turned from the one to the other, searching for the connexion between the stranger and the King he served, not liking this new alliance.

'Your Majesty cannot have considered this,' he muttered.

'I think my words were plain enough.'

'Has the Princess agreed to this?'

Richard obviously decided to ignore the aggressive manner the Earl was adopting.

'She does not know of it yet. But how can she refuse? To know this bond will sheath the swords of half the world. . .? To stem the blood, bind up the wounds and heal a host of men, and give them lives and futures . . .? Now there's a marriage contract which puts sacrifice to shame and makes a Saint of any woman.'

The Doctor was pleased at the force of Richard's argument and nodded in agreement, avoiding the unpleasant look the Earl was directing at him.

'Who gave you this idea, Sire?' asked Leicester directly.

'It came into my head.'

'It's utter madness!'

The King stared at him coldly, but this didn't deter the bitter flow of words in any way.

'Your Majesty, with all the strength at my command, I urge you to abandon this pretence of peace. . . .'

'Why?' interrupted the Doctor.

'Why?' echoed Leicester angrily. 'I'll tell you why! Because we are here to fight these Saracens and destroy them, not marry with them and make them our friends and relations.'

'This is an opportunity to save the lives of men. Why won't you even consider it?'

Richard stood listening as his two companions quarrelled, thankful to be relieved of the difficulties. It wasn't any fear of the Earl of Leicester which made the revelation of his plan a nervous business. Richard was afraid of no man. His great problem was that he knew the arguments Leicester would have on his side – for both were true fighting men – arguments for which he had, if the truth be told, a greater sympathy than the peaceful solution he was advocating.

'I speak as a soldier!' shouted Leicester, glaring at the Doctor, his eyes nearly starting out of their sockets with rage. 'Why are we here in this foreign land, if not to fight!' He turned to the King, emphasizing his words with a clenched fist. 'Sire, the Devil's Horde, Saracen and Turk possess Jerusalem. Have you forgotten that? We won't wrest that city from them with honeyed words, or smiles and artifice.'

The Doctor said, 'With swords, I suppose.'

'Aye, with swords, and lances – or the axe!'

A passion of fury overtook the Doctor, whose detestation for the slaughter of war overrode all his other emotions.

'You stupid butcher,' he stormed. 'Don't you know anything else but killing?'

'Oh, you're a man for a talk, I can see that,' sneered Leicester. 'You like a table and a ring of men. A parley here, arrangements there; documents, treaties . . . but when you men of State have stunned each other with your words, we . . . we, the fighting men, the soldiers, have to face it out.

And some half started morning while you speakers lie abed, armies settle everything . . . giving sweat and sinew, bodies, aye! and life itself to right the confusion of the council rooms.'

'I admire bravery, sir,' murmured the Doctor mildly, 'and bravery and courage are clearly in you in full measure. Unfortunately, you have no brains at all. I despise fools.'

Leicester pulled his sword free and advanced on the Doctor.

'A fool can match a coward any day!'

Richard stepped across and smashed his clenched fist down on Leicester's sword arm, numbing the muscles so that the fingers lost their strength and the weapon clattered to the stone floor.

'Do you dare flourish arms before your King?' He spat out, his body tense with anger. Leicester realized he had gone too far, muttered some words of apology and rubbed his arm.

'We have decided on this marriage pact with Saladin,' continued the King, in a clipped, formal voice. 'If it fails, my Lord of Leicester, then, and only then, shall we have a trial of arms. You have my permission to withdraw.'

Leicester gave a short, curt bow and, brushing the Doctor to one side deliberately, strode towards the door.

'And, Leicester,' murmured the King after him, 'my sister knows nothing of this. Remember that.'

As soon as they were alone, Richard gave a sigh and sat in a chair moodily.

'Do you think he will accept the idea?'

'He has no alternative, Sire,' replied the Doctor. 'It will rest easier with him if the plan succeeds, of course.'

'And it must succeed! Saphadin desires it, and Joanna will do as I tell her. All rests with this strange enemy of mine, this Saladin, this mixture of friend and foe. I long to hear his decision.' He smiled slightly at the Doctor, running a hand through his red hair. 'I can embrace him as a brother, or meet him on the field as a dangerous rival. Neither of these I fear. But, oh, how I detest the weary business of waiting.'

The two brothers who opposed Richard were considering the proposition at that very moment in Ramlah. Saladin sat on his favourite couch, reading the parchment which contained the offer of the marriage, while Saphadin, who had already read it, stood beside him. Saladin laid the document beside him at last, smiling slightly.

'A very entertaining proposition, brother.'

'Why do you smile? Is it a trap?'

'No, the English Malec Ric writes sincerely.' Saladin suddenly laughed quietly. 'It is so guileless, it can only be genuine.'

'Think seriously about it,' insisted Saphadin. 'Alliance with Joanna would give me title to much land, power over far-off countries . . . a glittering empire . . .'

'I did not know,' interrupted Saladin gently, 'that you were so ambitious.' Saphadin shifted his shoulders uneasily.

'I would be the name . . . yours would be the voice.'

'Ah!'

Saladin glanced at his brother quizzically for a second or two. 'Do not look so troubled. See, I will humour you and let this proposition go ahead.' Before his brother could open his mouth to thank him, Saladin tapped one finger into the palm of his other hand, dropping his voice so that his words were attended to carefully. 'But listen to me well. I see this marriage plan as no more than the end of an uneasy peace. Malec Ric is, as I say, sincere. But his mind is like the shifting sands. If it goes ahead, I will support it, to the hilt. But, brother, I beg of you not to rely on it coming to this favourable end.'

'Then you do think that Malec Ric is trying to make fools of us, or trick us?'

'I think this. That war is a mixture of many things. How

long the march, how short the battle. Strategy is worth a hundred lances. Think, brother. How does this offer help us?'

Saphadin sat down opposite his brother, giving him all his attention. Saladin spoke with considerable logic.

'Have England, France and all the rest come here to cheer a love match? So many men-at-arms, ships, horses; with all the armaments of war? I say this is a gesture of peace from a weary man. But weary men can rest and rise invigorated . . . so you reply softly to the letter while I call sharply to our forces. Dress yourself in finery; I'll see our men buckle on their swords. Practise your love words; I'll have our armies rehearse their war cries. Then on the day of wedding or the day of war we'll be prepared.'

What Richard would have thought if he could have overheard this conversation is more than any man can say. He might have admired the caution, while he welcomed the chance of success. But in any case in a few short hours the whole grand plan for peace was shredded into pieces and blown away. For there was one factor the King had overlooked.

Joanna.

Richard had been practising sword play with one of his friends, Hugh of Corillion, in a small enclosed sun-trap within the Palace. The exercise pleased Richard and when it was over he stripped off his dusty clothes, damp with the sweat of his exertions, and suffered his servants to throw sea-water over him while he rubbed at the muscles of his arms, legs and shoulders until they tingled. Totally refreshed, and very much at peace with the world, he put on a loose robe that reached down to his ankles and strolled back to his reading-room, intending to devote the rest of the day to the tiresome dispatches from England and the problem of his brother John, ruling there in his place during his absence, and obviously plotting against him.

The council chamber through which he had to pass

contained three people, but it was at Joanna he stared; the presence of the Doctor and the Earl of Leicester only just registering. The girl turned her head slowly as he entered and there was a hard, fierce intensity deep inside the centre of her eyes, which made them burn like tiny embers in an open fire. The skin of her face was parchment white, except for two spots of red high up on her cheek-bones. There was a flat, heavy feeling about the room and it took no great brain-work on the King's part to recognize trouble. His feet slowed to a stop and for the first time he glanced at the two men. Leicester looked uncomfortable but strangely triumphant, while the Doctor's face was grave and troubled.

'What's this I hear, Richard?' the girl said, her voice crackling with suppressed emotion. 'Marriage with that heathenish man! That infidel!'

Richard's heart sank. 'Joanna, there are many good reasons . . .'

'And when, pray, was I to hear the reasons? Afterwards? Is this what you do – throw off your sister and then explain?'

'It is expedient . . .'

'This unconsulted partner has no wish to marry! I am no sack of flour to be given in exchange. I am no paragraph in a peace treaty!'

'The decision has been made . . .'

'Not by me, and never would be. Never shall be!' Joanna took three or four little steps towards him, the whole of her body expressing her agitation and fury. 'How dare you do this, Richard!'

He held up his hands placatingly. 'Sister, I beg of you, consider. The war is full of weary, wounded men. This marriage wants a little thought from you, that's all and then you'll see the right of it.'

'And how would you have me go to Saphadin?' she cried furiously. 'This handsome hero you've selected; this peerless knight; this gentleman? Bathed in oriental perfume, I

98

suppose. Suppliant, tender and affectionate; soft-eyed and trembling with adoration! Eager with a thousand words of compliment and love!'

She shook her head so violently, her hair became disarrayed, some of it falling down the side of her face and spreading out over her bodice.

'But I like a different way, Richard – to meet the man I am to wed; to talk to him, learn about his ways, his moods and temperament; and show him mine.'

'If it's a meeting you want . . .'

'I do *not* want,' she flamed, determined not to allow him to get his words out. 'I will not have it!'

'I urge you to accept, Joanna.'

'No!'

Richard sighed and tried another approach. 'Very well, I entreat you.'

'No!'

Richard took her by the arm, a new note of authority entering his voice.

'I am the King. I command you.'

She pulled herself away. 'You cannot command this of me. There is a higher authority than yours to which I answer.'

'Where is there any man who has more power over his subjects?' he said aggressively. 'I am the King.'

Joanna said, 'Look to Rome.'

Richard stared at her, the awful realization of what she implied seeping through him.

'You would defy me and seek protection of the Pope?' he whispered.

'You defy the world,' she retorted, 'the world we know, at least. The very reason you are here in Palestine is the reason on my side. Are you not here to recapture the Holy City; fight the heathen invaders? If you marry me to one of them, Richard, you make a pact with the Devil. No, I'll never do it, never! Force me to it, and I'll turn the whole world into your enemy. Yours will be a hated shadow, even to your family and friends. I swear that I will demand of His Holiness that he bring down upon you the brand of excommunication!'

Her brother stared at her, his mouth dropping open in astonishment.

'You . . . you would not dare, Joanna.'

'Beware, Richard. You have met your match this day.'

Joanna swept out of the room, leaving the startled, mortified King and his two silent companions to their thoughts. Richard sat down slowly in a chair, passing a hand over his forehead, a dozen ideas chasing each other round his brain. Then suddenly a pure and blinding anger drove everything from his mind. His whole scheme lay in ruins and his personal pride had taken a knock in the bargain, for he knew quite certainly that he could never force the issue with his sister. He fixed his gaze malevolently on the Doctor.

'This ill-timed news,' he growled, 'I could have brought it to her slowly. Who gave away my plan?'

The Doctor took an anxious step forward.

'Your Majesty, you must believe . . .'

'Go!' the King screamed, so that the room echoed with the noise of his voice. 'Get out of my sight. You are not welcome here!'

The Doctor bowed coldly and walked out of the room, conscious of the smiling face of his adversary, the Earl of Leicester. He was desperately aware that what had been a peaceful haven, a most reliable refuge for him and Vicki, while Ian went in search of Barbara, had now become a place full of menace, where at any moment hands might descend and drag the pair of them away and thrust them into some dark dungeon from which they might never emerge.

He hurried to Vicki's bedroom, where he found her admiring one of the dresses Ben Daheer had had made for

her, holding it up against herself and walking about the room. She ran to him immediately, holding it out for his approval, then fell silent as she saw his face.

'Vicki, my child,' he said rapidly, 'we are in the utmost danger. We must leave Jaffa at once. Take what things you need, put on a dark cloak and follow me.'

'Why, Doctor? What's happened?'

'That infernal meddler, the Earl of Leicester, told the Princess about King Richard's plans to marry her to Saladin's brother. The King thinks I have given him away. Come along now. We haven't any time to waste.'

Vicki obediently put down the dress, clipped on a cloak which covered her page's outfit almost completely and ran after the Doctor. The two of them made their way hurriedly through the Palace, taking the least-used corridors, and passing rooms with open doorways as unobtrusively as they could.

'Where are we going?' she asked him breathlessly as they walked out of the Palace, past the guards and into the town of Jaffa itself. Then he stood with her in a doorway.

'Back to the wood, my dear,' he said grimly. 'Back to the *Tardis*. We'll be safe there, and Chesterton is a man with his wits about him. He'll realize that's where we are and follow us with Barbara.'

He turned and looked back at Richard's palace. He watched as a servant ran out and spoke to one of the guards outside, asking him some question or other. The guard nodded and pointed to the direction he and Vicki had taken. The servant then began to run back into the Palace, as fast as his legs would carry him. The Doctor stepped swiftly out of the doorway, urging Vicki round a corner, into a side street.

'That servant was asking if we'd left the Palace, wasn't he?' the girl said, half running to keep up with the Doctor's long strides.

'Yes, my dear, I'm afraid you're probably right. But we'll be safe in the *Tardis*, I promise you. If we ever get there,' he added under his breath.

CHAPTER SIX

The Triumph of El Akir

Haroun ed Diin had overheard the news that El Akir was returning to Lydda, and now he crouched on top of a half-ruined building of that town, alerted at the sight of the two horses galloping fast down the hillside. He eased his cramped muscles, for he had been waiting for nearly four hours, since he had learned the news about his hated enemy's expected arrival, wanting every part of him to respond to action when his brain commanded. The two horses swept out of sight for a moment behind a grove of trees, and the waiting man picked up the bow and arrow which lay on the flat roof beside him, wondering who the other rider with El Akir was, how it concerned his plans. He looked now at the entrance gates to the Emir's Palace. Guards were already running (he could see quite clearly over the white walls which enclosed the Palace grounds) and in a moment the great doors were swung open. Haroun noted the guards. Two now taking up positions outside, three more within, while a Captain superintended – six altogether. He wondered whether it was going to be possible to shoot his arrow at El Akir and make his retreat, and ran over his escape route once again in his mind.

The roof of the house upon which he lay, hiding behind a three-foot parapet which ran all the way around its four sides, adjoined, behind him, to another. He planned to cross the rooftops, swing down on a knotted rope he had secured firmly to the adjoining house, run across a small alley-way and lose himself in the tangle of houses and shops on the other side. It was getting across that alley that was going to be the most dangerous.

Haroun picked up the bow and fitted the shaft to it carefully. The only reason to be alive, after he had killed El Akir, was his youngest daughter Safiya. If they caught him . . . well, they would catch him and kill him and that would be the end, and Safiya would have to fend for herself. There was no question of his putting off his plan. He'd already had to wait for nearly a year.

The two horses came into view again and the man on the roof picked out the details of El Akir's travelling companion: the costume, the way she clung so desperately to the horse and the ropes binding her hands. So El Akir had found himself another victim, thought Haroun. Again the two horses disappeared as they entered the outskirts of Lydda and houses intervened, and now came the most difficult part. Haroun dared not show himself above the parapet in case one of the guards spotted him and gave the alarm. He had to trust to his ears to tell him when the horse brought El Akir near enough for him to be a certain target. He lay down patiently, tensing his legs slightly.

The sound of the horses' hooves came nearer, riding fast up the street. Haroun edged his head upwards and risked a look over the parapet. He had judged the time absolutely, except that El Akir had now drawn his prisoner's horse parallel with his, so that the girl's body was accidentally interposed. Haroun decided he must take every possible chance and sat up, clearly in view to anyone who cared to look upwards, but the guards were busy concentrating on the Emir's arrival, bunching now in the gates.

El Akir jumped off his horse and Haroun raised the bow, but again, as if Fate were determined to interfere, one of the guards moved and made the target impossible. Haroun ground his teeth in anger and then forgot his own vendetta for the moment. El Akir had hold of a rope tied to his prisoner's wrists and he deliberately wrenched on it, so that the girl was pulled off her mount and sent crashing to the hard, sunbaked earth. The guards laughed as the girl shook her head wearily and, although obviously dazed by the fall, tried to pick herself up. She was almost on her feet when she staggered and fell again, lying still this time, a pathetic, crumpled heap on the ground. Haroun felt a rush of pity for the unfortunate girl – then remembered his reason for being where he was and watched furiously as El Akir walked through the big gates and disappeared out of sight, flanked by three of his guards and the Captain. Before he went, he ordered the remaining two soldiers to bring the girl.

Haroun let go of the bow and arrow in disgust and was just about to retrace his steps to safety when he noticed the girl make a tiny movement with her head and realized that she was only shamming unconsciousness. The two guards were obviously making some joke about her, probably to do with the treatment she could expect from their master. He watched as the two men strolled over to the girl, one moving towards her feet, the other bending down to take hold of her bound wrists. Suddenly, with a speed and an agility which almost took Haroun's breath away, the girl kicked out with her feet into the face of the guard behind her and simultaneously dug her fingers into the other guard's face. Both men fell and in an instant she was on her feet, running for all she was worth.

In a second, Haroun bent double and ran across the roof, leaving the bow and arrow where they were for another time. He crossed to the other house to where he had fixed his rope and was just in time to see the girl running down the little alley-way with the two soldiers in hot pursuit.

He stood, crouched beside his rope now, wondering if the men would notice it, urging the girl silently on as she rushed towards the very passage-way he had marked down for his own flight, her tightly-bound hands held out in front and her hair flowing behind her. She had long since lost her yashmak and Haroun could see the cruel gag which stretched her mouth open. He saw the loose stone ahead of her and almost shouted to warn her, but in a second her foot had caught on it and she fell badly, knocking all the breath out of her body as her shoulder struck the ground. The two guards, who had seen their quarry almost disappear into the safety of the maze of houses, their brains shuddering at what their master would do to them, gave a shout of joy and ran towards her.

Haroun swung himself up to the little parapet and launched himself into the air. His two feet struck the guards equally, right in the centre of each of their backs, sending them both staggering with the force of the unexpected attack. Haroun fell to the ground, rolled and jumped to his feet, conscious that the girl was staring at him in astonishment. He rushed over to the dazed men, who had bumped into each other and fallen into an untidy heap, heaved them up and banged their heads together violently, watching in satisfaction as they rolled away and lay still. He moved over to the girl and gently brought her to her feet.

Barbara stared at her rescuer curiously as he untied her hands and removed the gag from her mouth. She saw a strong, compact man of just over six foot, poorly dressed in patched clothes. Yet, for all his poverty of dress, there was a certain dignity and bearing about him; and while lines of deep sadness had cut their way into his face, his eyes had a genuine humour. Barbara guessed his age to be in the early forties. Instinctively she felt she could trust him.

He took her by the arm firmly and guided her through the passage-way, hurrying her through this arch and down that turning, until her sense of direction floundered.

'I am Haroun ed Diin,' he told her.

'Thank you for helping me. But why did you?'

'We have a common enemy in El Akir. It makes for uncommon friendship.'

'Where are we going?'

'To safety. My daughter, Safiya, will give you something to eat and drink. Then you will sleep, restfully, knowing that I am on guard.'

'Something to drink sounds marvellous,' she said gratefully.

'It will help to wash away the taste those carrion must have left in your mouth.'

Barbara noticed that they were moving into a much poorer and more depressing part of the town. Where before the occasional people they had passed had eyed her curiously, now the glances were bolder, sharper, much more inquisitive. The dwellings were more tightly packed, making a rabbit warren of alleys and corridors.

'Since Lydda has been in the grip of El Akir,' Haroun told her, 'all manner of people are poor. But in the Old Quarter, where we are now, the sweepings of the area are gathered. Thieves, villains, cut-throats, these are my neighbours – some of them my friends.'

'Yet you are not one of them?'

He shook his head, a wry smile on his face. 'Not truly, although I have adopted some of their ways this last year. There is one consolation. El Akir's soldiers do not come to the Old Quarter.'

He drew her through an old, crumbling archway and up a winding flight of stone stairs, the steps worn down by many feet. His hand at her elbow he guided her carefully, pointing out the pitfalls, helping her where the stones were damaged.

Finally, he stopped at a door upon which he knocked once, paused and knocked twice again, pushed it open and led her into a small hallway, composed of three blank walls in a bad state of repair and an arched entrance covered with a curtain of beads. He stepped over to the arch and held the strings of beads aside, gesturing to her to enter.

'My poor house is yours,' he said softly.

Barbara walked through and found quite the opposite to what she had expected, for the room beyond was beautifully clean (although she had anticipated this, at least, from her estimation of the man) and furnished well. The carpet under her feet was soft and so far beyond his means that she wondered if it were stolen. And yet she put the idea out of her head, because Haroun didn't seem to fit the role of thief, even in the face of his having said he had borrowed some of his neighbours' habits.

A girl opened a door and walked into the room and Haroun went to meet her, taking her hands and kissing her on the forehead.

'This is my daughter, Safiya.'

She was perhaps sixteen or seventeen, with a slender figure and a beautiful heart-shaped face, physically a perfectly-formed woman, yet with the innocence and mannerisms of a child, and her pleasure at seeing Barbara was one of completely unaffected delight. She ran over and hugged her, and Haroun gave Barbara a grave smile above his daughter's head.

'Safiya welcomes company other than mine.'

'Oh, Father, that is not true! You know I love you dearly.' She looked up into Barbara's face, for she stood less than five feet. 'But I do hope your visit will be a long one. For a moment, Father, I thought you had found Maimuna.'

Haroun's face suddenly revealed a tremendous sadness, and he turned away.

'No, I have had no fortune with my search today, Safiya.'

The girl disengaged herself from the embrace and led Barbara to a couch, chattering about her thoughtlessness in keeping Barbara on her feet, and asking her if she would like something to eat and drink.

'Yes, bring our guest some refreshment. Treat her as you would a close cousin, daughter. And bring clear water, as well as wine,' said Haroun.

'Yes, Father,' Safiya replied obediently. She took Barbara's hands and examined the weals on her wrists with dumb horror, her eyes widening and filling with tears.

'They look much worse than they are,' said Barbara gently.

'I'll prepare some food, and then we must bathe them – I have some salve which I shall spread on your wounds as soon as you have eaten.' She looked up at Barbara. 'You have not told me your name,' she said timidly.

'Barbara.'

The girl kissed Barbara's hands and ran out of the room. Haroun drew up a stool and sat down.

'Haroun, I don't want to make trouble for you and your daughter. You've done more than enough for me already, getting me away from El Akir's men.'

He held up a hand as she spoke. 'I am in constant danger,' he said seriously. 'A man who seeks vengeance always is. For I have sworn to take the life of him who has destroyed all that I hold most dear.'

'El Akir?'

'Yes, that vile and evil creature. Last year I lived some eight days' ride from here, in a prosperous little town, near the river of Litani. I had a reputation as an honest trader, organizing caravans from the coastal towns of Tripoli and Beirut to Syria and Egypt. At that time I was accounted rich, but my real wealth lay in a gentle, devoted wife, a son who honoured and obeyed me and two daughters who adorned whatever place they visited. We lived in a fine house, filled with laughter and happiness.'

Barbara sat quietly, giving the man every scrap of her attention. He spoke undramatically, not colouring his words with any undue emphasis or emotion, as if he were relating events which had occurred to someone else.

'One day,' he continued, 'to that town of Selnik where I resided with my family, El Akir came to trade. He and his men had captured a Venetian ship that had gone aground near the coastal town of Sidon, which lies between Beirut and Tyre. He boasted how he had crept down to the beaches, slain the sailors who were trying to save the ship's cargo, and transported the stolen goods overland. The prices he asked were four times as much as the goods were worth and of the first three traders he visited two he slaughtered and one he had beaten so badly he was crippled for life – for all three refused to do business with him. Then he came to me. I had been warned about the man, and called out my friends and servants. Together we disarmed his men and drove them from the town. El Akir we carried, ignoring his screams for mercy, and dropped him in the River Litani and made him a laughing-stock. Hundreds lined the bank as the villain splashed and spluttered.'

'You should have killed him then,' said Barbara.

'Perhaps, but at that time the punishment seemed the right one.'

The rattling of cooking utensils and the pattering of Safiya's feet in the kitchen broke the silence that fell between them. Barbara waited, knowing she must hear the end of Haroun's story, realizing that perhaps he was relating it all for the first time and that the very telling of it might help to ease his private sorrows.

'I had to leave Selnik to visit my business friends in Tripoli and I took Safiya with me, for I believed that travel sharpened the imagination of my children, so each one was my companion, in rotation, on my journeys. El Akir had now collected a small army. He descended on Selnik and burned my house, put my wife and son to the sword, sold my servants into slavery. My warehouses, livestock, vineyards, all were destroyed. And when he left this death and destruction and came to Lydda he brought my other daughter, Maimuna, with him.'

'Wasn't there anything you could do, Haroun? No law to protect you?'

'None. For the great battles take precedent over minor

incidents such as mine. So, when I learned of the tragedy this awful man had visited upon me, I brought Safiya to Lydda, adopted this disguise and waited my turn – I am still waiting.'

A little shiver ran down Barbara's back as she saw the intensity which had crept into his eyes, making them glitter. Then Safiya came in, bearing a pitcher of water and some plain goblets and broke the mood. Soon the three of them settled down to their evening meal.

El Akir, of course, was quite unaware of the presence of Haroun ed Diin in Lydda, or that he had become Barbara's unexpected ally. As a matter of fact, he had forgotten all about the incident at Selnik, for all the women in his harem had been taken by force and there were a considerable number of them, so Haroun's daughter Maimuna, even though her beauty was considerable, represented no more than another triumph in a chain of incidents to the Emir. He thought of them, collectively, as the advertisement of his power, as a true fighting man might count the number of his victories or a general add up the battles he had won.

As the Emir stared down at the two guards who had been responsible for Barbara's escape, the runaway became the symbol of setback, and his vanity couldn't accept such a thing. His ingenuity had led to the girl's abduction, right under the nose of the Great Sultan himself. Now she had gone because of the stupidity of two lazy, inefficient members of his Palace guard. They had been brought before him and stuttered out the story. A dozen men, they swore, had attacked them and carried the girl off, each one of the men being seven feet in height and heavily armed. El Akir didn't waste any time considering the excuses. He turned to the Captain of his guard.

'Their punishment is your affair, Abu Talib, but see that it is harsh. I have no use for fools.'

Abu Talib spoke a few words and the two guards were pulled away, screaming and protesting.

'They will be flayed, master, until they reveal the real truth of what occurred. Then they will be imprisoned . . . with a cask of water.'

El Akir studied the face of his Captain sharply and Abu Talib smiled slowly.

'The cask of water will have a large amount of salt added to it!'

The Emir nodded, dismissing the matter from his mind.

'Now the girl! What has been done to bring her back?'

'We have searched Lydda for her and can find nothing.'

'All of Lydda?'

'All but the Old Quarter, but that is a den of thieves, Your Excellency. I would need many men.'

'Take every man you require,' shouted El Akir. 'I want every room in every place searched. Throw light on every shadow. Tell the men I will pay fifty gold pieces for the woman, but tell them she must be found.'

Abu Talib put his right hand over his heart, bowed and hurried away. Half an hour later, a hundred men descended on their objective from four sides, separated into groups of twenty-five, while another fifty men with the Captain at their head marched to the very centre of the Old Quarter and set themselves down in a crumbling old square, ready to strike at any place should there be any serious resistance.

Barbara awoke to find Haroun shaking her shoulder. Immediately she heard the distant sounds of shouts and running feet and quickly sat up on the couch. Safiya stood near her, trembling with agitation.

'The soldiers have invaded the Old Quarter,' Haroun said quietly.

'It's my fault,' she replied, shaking the sleep from her head. 'They've come to search for me.'

'You will be safe here. I have a hiding-place.'

He turned and nodded to his daughter, who ran obediently to one of the walls and tugged on a rope which hung from the ceiling. Barbara watched as part of the wall

moved outwards, revealing a small cubby-hole. Safiya
stepped inside it and melted into the shadows.

'There isn't room for three of us in here,' Barbara
objected. Haroun took out the knife he wore in his belt and
held it out to her.

'I go out into the streets, my lady. I shall find a way the
soldiers have not discovered, return and conduct you and
Safiya through their lines. But take this knife. If you are
careful, no one will discover you. But should the soldiers
search too diligently, Safiya must not fall into their hands.'

Barbara stared at the knife in her hands, a feeling of
horror invading her.

'Kill her?' she whispered. Haroun nodded grimly.

'Yes, and then yourself.'

'No!'

'You must,' he insisted, closing her hand around the hilt.

'Maimuna lives, in degradation and misery. Safiya must not know that sort of future.'

'I couldn't do it, Haroun, I couldn't!' she whispered helplessly.

'You would not let them take Safiya?'

'No.'

'You know what El Akir is like?'

She gazed up at him, a mute appeal in her eyes, finding no remorse in his for what he was asking of her, no single indication he would ever change his mind. He laid a hand on top of her head, gazing at her steadily, as if to transmit his purpose to her both mentally and physically. Then he turned on his heel and left her.

Safiya crept out of the opening and ran to Barbara, pulling at her sleeve urgently.

'Come, Barbara, I beg of you. We must hide. See, we have the hiding-place, and Father has left a knife to defend ourselves with.'

Barbara let herself be led across the room and through the opening in the wall. Safiya pulled on a handle and closed the door, pushing a piece of wood through the handle so that the door couldn't be opened from the outside. The two girls then sank down on the cushions which covered the floor – placed there for just such an emergency – the older one putting her arms around the younger, while the sounds in the streets below, although fainter to them because of their enclosure, actually began to get closer.

Haroun ed Diin slipped out of his front door and ran silently down the worn steps towards the shouts and the cries. He had abandoned his shoes and left them in the little hall, needing every possible protection silence could afford. But he was unfortunate. He ran straight into a body of soldiers at the bottom of the stairs and, before he could stop himself, they saw him. He tried desperately to turn and go back the way he had come, but it was too late. One of the soldiers crashed the hilt of his sword on the unlucky man's head and Haroun staggered to one side and fell through a window, smashing the rickety shutters and plunging into the room beyond. The soldiers peered in after him, ready to put down any resistance, but when they saw his still body lying amidst the debris of the shutters, they moved away laughing, walking up the stairway, hammering on any doors they came across and breaking them down if they weren't immediately opened. The same thing was happening throughout the Old Quarter. Sometimes a man would join up with one or two friends and wage a running battle but the soldiers were too many and too well armed.

The two girls suddenly froze into absolute stillness as they heard a thunder of fists on the outer door, then a splintering of wood as it was kicked in violently. Then there was a rustle and clicking as the bead curtain was disturbed and two voices started talking very close to the hiding-place.

'You take the others and search higher up. I will make sure no one is concealed in the rest of this place.'

'Very well,' said the other voice, 'but if you find the woman, remember we have agreed to share the Emir's reward.'

Once again the bead curtain was disturbed. Barbara listened as footsteps moved across the room into the kitchen. She gripped hold of the knife in her hands, hoping against hope that the men would not be too careful and start examining the walls. She knew if they did that they would be bound to discover the cracks made by the secret door. A piece of crockery smashed to the ground in the kitchen, and Safiya clutched hold of Barbara, snuggling up against her in fright.

For the third time, Barbara heard the movement of the bead curtains, as the other man returned.

'There is nothing above,' the voice announced.

'Nothing here, either. You know, whoever lives here has a rich taste. Look at this carpet.'

'Stolen, I shouldn't wonder.'

'Then let's light a torch and burn the place. No reason why the villain should enjoy his crimes.'

The two men laughed.

Barbara put her lips close to Safiya's head.

'Crouch up against the corner,' she whispered.

'What are you going to do, Barbara?'

'Now stay here, Safiya. Do as I tell you! Lock the door after me, but as soon as I've gone, go out in the streets and find your father, for they may set light to the house. If you stay here you'll burn to death or suffocate.'

Barbara moved quietly to the piece of wood securing the door and withdrew it slowly. Then she pushed the door and stepped into the room. The two men, fortunately, had their backs to her, busily heaping cushions and some fabric they had found on the couch, intending to set light to it. Barbara moved quickly to the doorway then turned so that she stood

stepped back, stunned with the force of the blow, then a smile twisted his mouth.

'This defiance promises well for me. It means it will take a long time to make you scream for pity.' His voice dropped quietly, a shudder of pleasure running through him and Barbara felt a quiver of fear.

'I shall sit here and devise some entertainment for you. Take her to the harem,' he ordered the two guards, throwing them a purse from his belt. 'She will learn a little of what to expect from the other women there.' He turned his black, fathomless eyes to Barbara's again. 'But nothing will be so bad, so painful, so shaming, or so terrifying as what is to happen to you.'

For the first time in her life, Barbara fainted.

CHAPTER SEVEN

The Will of Allah

Ian left the small retinue which had accompanied him from Jaffa with strict instructions to sound out as much as they could about Saladin's opinion of King Richard's marriage proposals between his sister and the Sultan's brother, urging them to remember every detail and make the return to Jaffa as speedily as possible. Ian had already discovered that Saladin would not exchange Sir William des Preaux at any price, a point about which the Saracen leader was totally adamant. However, he promised that the Knight would be well treated and that he would reconsider his decision at some future date, and with that Ian had to be content. Saladin, did, however, lend a most favourable ear to Ian's plea for permission to follow El Akir and rescue Barbara. Much as he might not wish to quarrel with a potential ally, Saladin had no objection to a third party intervening, though he confessed that Ian stood very little chance on his own. His acute sense of judgement told him that Ian would have to be forcibly restrained, so he ordered that a clearance be given to him to travel unmolested to Lydda, plus a declaration that Ian and 'the lady, Barbara', should have a safe journey back to Jaffa.

'I give you these passes,' he told Ian, 'because I admire your bravery and courage, Sir Ian. Secondly, the lady Barbara had believed she was under my protection and I would have that belief honoured. Lastly, El Akir has presumed upon my situation in this war, and his value to me in it, and I would have that rectified. His main army, of four thousand men, it is true, is placed with the body of my fighting men in front of Jerusalem, but he has a personal guard in Lydda of several hundred. One thing and one thing alone can bring success to your enterprise . . . the Will of Allah.' He smiled at Ian wryly.

'But of course, you are a Christian, and my words mean nothing to you.'

'On the contrary, Your Highness, if you will forgive my contradicting you, the names and the phrases differ but the purpose is the same in all races of intellect and culture. You say "the Will of Allah" where we would say "the Hand of God".'

'I see you have made some study of the subject, young man,' murmured Saladin approvingly, 'but surely the conflict still remains? The gulf between our separate faiths is too wide to be bridged by such a simple explanation.'

'I have a friend, a very wise, well-travelled man who spoke to me on the subject of religions once. In the West, three main streams dominate: Mohammedanism, Judaism and Christianity. In the East, the Hindu, the Buddhist and the Moslem rival Janism, Sikhism, Parsee and Shinto. But what is the sum total? That all people, everywhere, believe there is something mightier than themselves. Call it Brahma, Allah or God – only the name changes. The little Negro child will say his prayers and imagine his God to be in his colour. The French child hopes his prayers will be answered – in French. We are all children in this matter still, and will always be – until colours, languages, custom, rule and fashion find a meeting ground.'

'Then why do we fight? Throw away life, mass great continents of men and struggle for opposing beliefs?'

Neither could provide an answer so Ian took his leave as decently as he could, although Saladin was now keen for him to stay and hear the arguments put forward by the many wise men and philosophers who filled his court. Ian's only regret was that he had had to speak for the Doctor and knew that his friend would eternally regret not meeting the great Sultan.

He rode hard out of Ramlah, following much the same route that El Akir and Barbara had taken, until the fierce heat of the sun warned him how unused he was to the climate. His horse's head was weaving slightly from side to side, its body covered with lather, and finally he reined the animal on top of an incline and gazed round the country-side. Nothing stirred in the merciless heat which had by no means risen to its peak. The land was quarter desert, tracts of sand broken by hard-baked ground, occasional scrub grass and here and there little clumps of trees. It looked like a dead world. He urged his horse towards one of the nearest clumps of trees, where he knew he would find a water pool. For a moment he thought he saw a movement but then, when he searched the place with his eyes and saw no other signs of life, took it to be imagination.

He dismounted near the trees, leading the horse gratefully through them, both man and animal enjoying the shade. The horse was flaring its nostrils now, smelling the water ahead and needed no urging. Soon, both came to a small pool of crystal-clear water. Ian bent down and scooped some of it into his face, enjoying the trickles that ran down his neck and under his clothes. Then he drank with cupped hands and moved away to the shadiest spot he could find and sat down. His horse lapped at the water then raised its head, shuffling its hooves uncomfortably.

'What is it, old chap?' asked Ian. The horse stood absolutely still, except for a slight movement of its ears, and Ian had an immediate sensation that someone's eyes were watching him. He started to get to his feet, his hand reaching for the sword at his side, when something hit him a sickening blow on the back of his neck. For a second he believed he could fight the pain and the dizziness and tried to get to his feet, but then everything was blotted out in a sparkle of light that flashed from somewhere behind his eyes, and he started to fall. Before he touched the ground he was completely unconscious.

A moment later, it seemed to him, his eyelids fluttered open and he was aware of the dull ache at the base of his skull. He tried to get up and found that he had been pegged out, away from the little oasis, lying directly underneath the full power of the sun. He realized he must have been unconscious for some time because all his clothes had been removed except for his trousers and boots. He tugged at the ropes around his wrists without any success then tried to move his legs, but they were also very firmly secured.

He closed his eyes tightly to shut out the overhead glare. His mouth was dry and the perspiration the sun had drawn from his naked chest had long since dried. His whole body felt as if the skin had shrunk. He heard a movement from the direction of the grove of trees and turned his head.

A most extraordinary spectacle greeted his eyes, for shambling towards him was an Arab dressed in horrible looking rags which hung in such shreds on his body it was almost impossible to imagine their original shape and colour. The man had a frayed patch over one eye, which made him hold his head rather to one side, and in his hands he clutched a small jar with a stick of wood protruding from it.

'Ah! My Lord, you are awake,' he said, grinning with delight and showing a mouth full of broken teeth.

'I suppose you were the one who knocked me out?' asked Ian, even more conscious of how dry his mouth was.

'The same, the very same.'

'No chance that you'll untie me?'

The Arab looked at him in hurt surprise.

'Well, how about some water then?'

'Now that would be as rare to you as ivory, My Lord, I know it would. Of course, there is plenty of water – and it costs nothing at all.'

'Bring me some, then.'

'You see, it is the *carrying* of the water, My Lord. I would have to do that, and very difficult and arduous work it would be, too. What would you pay for such service?'

Ian restrained his temper, knowing it wouldn't do him any good to start shouting or blustering. It didn't seem to him as if threats were going to have any effect, either – not in this deserted part of the country, where the majority of people would be hiding in the shade.

'How much do you want?'

The Arab sat down on his knees with a chuckle of pleasure, for all the world as if he were about to start a conversation with a close friend.

'I am such a simple man. I want everything you have.'

'Now listen to me carefully . . .'

The Arab put on his most serious expression and bent forward attentively.

'Yes, My Lord.'

'I have no money with me . . .'

'That is a great pity.'

'But take me to Lydda and I will pay you there.'

The Arab sat back on his heels in absolute astonishment.

'You want to go to Lydda, My Lord?'

'Yes.'

'But that is a most peculiar thing.'

'Why?'

'Because,' he replied, with rising excitement, 'I live in Lydda.'

'You do?'

'Truly, I would not lie to you.'

'But this is very fortunate.'

'It is kismet, My Lord, there is no other way of explaining it.'

The Arab clapped his hands together with such pleasure and chuckled so loudly that a smile edged at the corner of Ian's lips, and he nearly forgot his own situation.

'Then you'll take me there?'

'I'm afraid I cannot, My Lord,' replied the Arab, with a heavy sigh of disappointment.

'But . . . but why not?'

'Because you are tied up on the sand here, you see, and it is such an expensive business to undo the knots . . . and you have no money.'

He smiled at Ian apologetically. Ian let his head rest back on the sand, realizing he had no simpleton to deal with.

'Then I shall just have to lie here and go mad in the sun, my friend, for all my money is in Lydda and that's that.'

The Arab peered at him with exaggerated anxiety.

'Surely, My Lord, you do not think I am such a terrible fellow as to spreadeagle you out in the sand like this just to deprive you of water, or to let the sun melt your mind into fantasy.' He clicked his tongue reproachfully. 'That is a very unworthy thought, My Lord, and it is not the sort of thing I expect from you at all.'

'Oh, I'm so sorry,' murmured Ian sarcastically.

'Quite right, because it is all very well for you. Here you are, fixed in this position and able to say what you like to me, and I can do nothing because you have no money. Really, My Lord, that is hardly my fault, now, is it?'

Ian glanced at the man blankly.

'Not your fault! Who put me here in the first place?'

'But what could I do? You arrive beside the water pool, and I can see you are a rich Lord, so I am tempted to knock you out and search your clothes. The temptation was your fault, for you are obviously rich and I am obviously poor. So I search through your clothes and I find nothing. Again, My Lord, am I at fault? I must earn my living and Allah has decided that my profession is to be a thief. I can tell you I was very frustrated, My Lord, very frustrated indeed.'

'So you tied me up?'

'I could scarcely leave you where you were. What profit is there in that? I would be a poor thief if I didn't do my job properly. Besides, you are much bigger and stronger than I am, and would undoubtedly attack me when you recovered if I didn't render you helpless.'

Ian thought it might be worth trying a threat or two, to see what this would do to the Arab's confidence.

'Now, listen, you scoundrel, I have papers personally signed by the Sultan himself at Ramlah, giving me free travel permission through this country.'

'I know, My Lord, and very important they look too. But only of value to you. My Lord, I *want* you to travel. I am most anxious for you to be happy and to do the things you have set your heart on doing.' He shrugged helplessly. 'It all is so expensive.'

'Take me to Lydda then.'

'Ah, I am cursed with the affliction of disbelief. And you have done me an injustice already, when you thought I had placed you out here on the sand for the tortures of sun or lack of water.'

Ian looked at him thoughtfully. The Arab held up the little pot he had placed beside him gleefully.

'A pot of honey, My Lord. Made from pounded dates, and very sweet. Now if you turn your head to the left you will see a mound. Look as closely as you can and you will be able to see little creatures hurrying and scurrying about. Oh, it is a hungry little home, My Lord, and its inhabitants go wild for honey.'

Ian turned his head sharply in horror and saw the mound not more than ten feet away from his outstretched left hand, which was firmly tied, like his other limbs, to a stake buried deep in the ground.

The Arab stepped across his body and knelt beside his left wrist.

'Now what we do is daub a little of the honey on your hand, My Lord, and spread a little trail to the ant-hill. And then I will retire to the shade of the trees and dream of the treasure you will give me – when the ants discover you.'

'I haven't any money,' Ian said sharply, trying to keep the panic out of his voice, 'I swear to you I haven't.'

The Arab ignored him and started to daub honey on Ian's hand with the stick and letting the runny mixture drip down on the sand in a line towards the ant-heap. Ian strained and struggled at the stakes in a vain attempt to wrench himself free, but the Arab had done his job too well, and in a moment Ian had to lie still, exhausted in every muscle. The Arab returned, still with the smile on his face, his one eye beaming out cheerfully.

'There we are, My Lord – all done. Now remember all you have to do is call me. I shall not be far away.'

He walked away to the trees and settled himself down in the shade of one of them, waving in a friendly fashion to Ian.

Ian turned his head and looked at the ant-heap. Already he could see a dark mass of the little insects investigating the honey at the base of their city, and one or two were moving now to investigate the sudden vein of fortune which had appeared from nowhere. Ian tore his eyes away and tried desperately to think. He wondered if he could get a purchase on either of his wrists by arching his body, and he tried it, so that just his head and his heels were touching the sand, but all it did was strain his muscles. Then he tried to turn on to his right side, hoping he could drag out his left hand, and the stake, by sheer sinew. But this attempt had just as much success. Obviously the Arab knew exactly what he was doing.

He suddenly felt a thrill of horror as something began to run over his hand and he turned his head quickly, his throat tightening in fear. The line of honey was nearly obscured now by the long, dark line of ants, all struggling and threshing, running and working away, transporting the honey back to the nest. Another ant ran over his fingers and he agitated his hand violently in a desperate attempt to shake them off or frighten them away. He knew it wasn't going to be any good. When they reached the end of the honey they would then be attracted to the salt in the pores of his skin and start digging for that. He imagined them gradually spreading up his arm, could almost hear the signals going back to the nest, calling for more workers to mine this rich harvest spread out so conveniently near. He pictured the wave of insects travelling slowly up his arm to his shoulder, fanning out on the plain of his chest. He felt them running along his neck and up his chin. He thought about them invading his mouth and his nostrils, packing into his ears ... his eyes.

His eyes.

It was that horror, that shuddering expectation of agony which made him cling on to the one faint hope he had.

He called out desperately to the Arab and felt a wave of relief as he saw the man jump up from the shade and shamble across to him.

'All right, I'll tell you. . . . I'll tell you where my money is,' he stammered, 'only keep them away . . . from me.'

The Arab stared down at him pensively and then nodded. He stepped across Ian's body and drew his battered shoe along the line of honey, rolling it and its seething mass of insect life back towards the ant-heap. Then he poured handfuls of sand over Ian's honey-coated hand and rubbed the sticky mess away.

'I can always start the process all over again,' he said seriously to Ian, 'if, of course, you are just making a fool of me. I do hope you are not, My Lord, because now I am quite excited and intrigued to know where this wealth of yours is kept.'

He stood over Ian, waiting.

'In my boot,' Ian muttered hoarsely, shaking his head from side to side, his eyelids drooping.

The Arab bent closer, not catching the words.

'Where, My Lord? You must speak a little louder.'

'The . . . the boot . . .' whispered Ian, and his head rolled to one side and lay still. The Arab clutched his head, as if he were berating himself for having overlooked such an obvious hiding-place and darted to Ian's right foot. He tore off the ropes hurriedly, glancing every so often at his prisoner, satisfying himself that he was indeed still in his faint. Then he pulled off the boot and thrust his hand deep inside it. He scrabbled about for a few seconds then threw it away in disgust. He hurried back to Ian, grabbed him by the hair and shook his head violently.

'You lied to me,' he said fiercely.

Ian opened his eyes gradually, blinking and having difficulty in focusing.

'The boot. . . .' he repeated.

'There is nothing there!'

'The . . . the left boot. . . .'

The Arab let go of his head and hurried to his left foot, tearing at the ropes, sitting astride the leg with his back to Ian. He was just starting to draw off the boot, when Ian drew back his right foot, aimed it at the centre of the Arab's back and straightened his leg.

It struck him right at the base of his spine like a ramrod, jarring the whole of his body and hurtling him forwards. Ian quickly drew up both legs and used them to lever his body upwards, tightening his hands around the stakes in the ground as he did so and heaving. The two pieces of wood were sucked out of the ground in a spray of sand and Ian staggered to his feet, just as the Arab shook himself and rose to his feet. For a moment the two men stared at each other, and the Arab made a dash for the trees. Ian ran across, the stakes tied to his wrists flailing around him dangerously, and hurled himself through the air in a flying tackle, catching the man around his waist and falling with him. In a second, Ian was on top of him, kneeling on his upper arms, his right hand gripping its tethered stake and holding it like a club.

'Lie still, or I'll split your skull open,' he said. The Arab stopped his futile struggling and relaxed.

'Don't kill me, My Lord,' he begged piteously.

'I'll think about it.'

'I am only a miserable thief. . . .'

'You're certainly miserable. Get these ropes off my hands.'

The thief obeyed hurriedly, talking crossly to the ropes, or cajoling them when they wouldn't move, smiling up at Ian as he worked, apologizing for the delay. Ian never took his eyes off him for a moment. Finally, the ropes fell away. Ian picked up one of the stakes and prodded the Arab lightly in the chest.

'What I ought to do is tie you down in the sand and let the ants eat you for dinner.'

'I would make a very poor meal for them, My Lord,' he replied seriously. 'Very tough flesh, mine, enough to give even an insect indigestion.'

Ian suppressed a smile. The Arab would cheerfully murder him if he turned his back, but there was an extra-ordinarily likeable quality about him.

'Take me to where you put my clothes.'

The Arab started to move towards the trees and Ian grabbed his arm.

'Don't move too quickly, my friend,'

'I was going to run and fetch your things for you, My Lord.'

'We'll both go.'

'Both go,' he repeated. 'Yes, of course, what an honour.'

The two men moved into the shade of the trees, where Ian found his clothes, neatly folded in a pile on top of his sword. He picked up the weapon and saw the Arab shrug his shoulders slightly, accepting the inevitable.

'You aren't afraid to die?' asked Ian curiously. The Arab shook his head. Ian pursed his lips and leaned both his hands on his sword, embedding its tip in the earth around the pool.

'Bring me some water. But don't try and run away. I

have no intention of killing you, unless you do something foolish.'

The Arab's face split open in a wide grin of delight and he scuttled over to a bush near by, where he had hidden some of his own belongings, produced a little clay bowl then hurried to the pool, filling it with water and bringing it to Ian.

Ian assuaged his thirst and poured the rest of the water over his body.

'You're going to take me to Lydda,' he stated. The Arab frowned.

'Not a very nice place,' he said.

'Why?'

'Full of thieves and villains.'

Ian laughed and the Arab joined him gleefully, clapping his hands together.

'I couldn't find anyone worse than you there,' said Ian.

'That is a great compliment, My Lord, and I am very grateful to you for it.'

'Do you know an Emir, by the name of El Akir?'

The change that came over the Arab was quite remarkable. A sudden watchfulness showed on his face, a slight tightening of the lips. He sat on the sand, his hands clasped around his knees, his one eye regarding Ian intently.

'You are a friend of the Emir, My Lord,' he asked casually, 'or a relative, perhaps?'

'No.'

'Ah, I understand. It is an army matter, and you carry orders from the great Sultan to him.'

'No.'

'Then it is a matter of business?'

'I have some business with El Akir, yes.'

There was a pause. 'You don't like him, do you?' said Ian, at last.

'My Lord, the Emir is a tyrant. He has made the rich so poor, there is no one left to steal from. But that is just one thing. In this world there are honest and dishonest men, good and bad, the pure and the evil. I have seen El Akir have children murdered in the public streets, watched as he laughed while young girls were tortured to death. I saw the Emir once himself commit the crime of hurling a man of religion from the top of a building, because he had objected to the way El Akir ill-treated the people.'

The Arab turned his head and stared into the quiet pool of water.

'Now I am a bad man, My Lord, very bad indeed, and I admit it. My father was a thief and his father before him. But all of us put together would make a purer man than El Akir can ever be.'

Ian nodded slowly. 'El Akir has abducted a friend of mine, a young lady. I am going to Lydda to get her back again – even if I have to kill him to do it.'

'Then I shall take you to Lydda, My Lord,' said the Arab quietly, 'and help you in any way I can.'

Ian had some doubts about this new alliance, but it certainly suited his purpose. He could hardly ride into the town and start asking where El Akir was without arousing suspicion; and then he had to find a way into the Emir's Palace, rescue Barbara and make his escape with her. He didn't for a moment underestimate the difficulties, so any kind of help was valuable, even if it had the strings of caution attached. The Arab had tethered Ian's horse near his own, which was the saddest creature Ian had ever seen, with ribs sticking out at its sides and a pair of huge, sorrowful eyes which seemed to bemoan its lot in life with silent constancy. Nevertheless, it was sturdier than it appeared to be and Ian had no complaint to make about their rate of progress, the Arab preceding him all the way. Neither could Ian find any cause for dissatisfaction in the trust he had given his new-found ally.

Finally, with the sky darkening as the sun fled from above, the Arab led Ian through a little pass of rocks and reined his panting horse, pointing ahead of him. Ian stopped beside him and stared at the town of Lydda lying ahead.

'We must move more slowly now,' said the Arab.

'What is your name?'

'Ibrahim, My Lord,' he said with a grin.

'Do you know any way I can get into El Akir's Palace, Ibrahim?'

The Arab shook his head. 'It is very well guarded and the wall is high. If you had gold you might bribe your way in. . . .'

'But I haven't any gold.'

The Arab chuckled loudly.

'Yes, that was a very good trick with the boots, My Lord. I must remember not to be taken in by it again.'

The two men urged their horses forward once again, picking their way slowly on the slight decline to the town, while Ian set himself the task of finding a way inside his enemy's stronghold.

Had he ridden faster he might have come across the two guards rushing Barbara through the streets towards the Palace, and speed of thought and instant action might have plucked Barbara away from them there and then. But Destiny had decreed the pattern of events otherwise.

Barbara came to her senses in a huge room decked out with tapestries and silk hangings, furnished with rich carpets and soft couches. A girl was bending beside her on the couch, bathing her face gently with scented water. Barbara stared at her for a moment or two, relishing the gentle touch of the hands on her face and the soothing quality of the water.

The girl was delicately formed, with full, generous lips and a pair of large and most expressive eyes. She stopped dabbing at Barbara's face, as she saw she had recovered and sat beside her on the couch, holding both her hands. Her resemblance to Safiya was quite remarkable.

'He is not here,' said the girl softly, anticipating the question trembling on Barbara's lips. 'Lie still and forget him, while you can.'

'Your name is Maimuna, isn't it?'

The girl stared at her in astonishment.

'How did you know that?' she cried. Barbara related her meeting with Maimuna's father, and her sister Safiya, and the story she had heard of the tragedy which had befallen the family of Haroun ed Diin. Maimuna finally covered her face with her hands, sobbing bitterly. Other girls began to move towards them, comforting the weeping girl and questioning Barbara about the cause of her unhappiness.

'I am not unhappy,' said Maimuna, through her tears, 'although the memory of that awful day when El Akir murdered my mother and brother and wrenched me from the home I loved is still almost more than I can bear. But I thought my father and my sister were dead too – for El Akir swore he had killed them.'

'They are alive, Maimuna,' said Barbara. 'You must believe me.'

The other girls wandered away again, disturbed at the mention of the tyrant's name, as if the only way they could exist was to shut him away from their minds on every possible occasion.

Each girl, Barbara noticed, was of a different race. One was a tall Negress, loose-limbed and very full of figure, wearing a multi-coloured costume and a pair of enormous bone earrings. Another was a slim, enchanting little Indian girl of no more than sixteen who walked with such dignity she seemed to glide over the floor, her pale-blue sari, edged with gold, emphasizing the grace of her body. There was a Turkish girl, older than the rest; a Persian beauty; a brown-skinned Syrian – each one a testament to beauty. But on all their faces was the mark of El Akir – the sad acceptance of enforced captivity and shame, for all were seized from their families by force, and each one had her private sorrow.

Of them all, Barbara thought Maimuna was the most attractive. Even the misery of enslavement had not marred her loveliness. There was an almost transparent quality about her skin and a depth of gentleness in her eyes. She had an air of shy tenderness about her which spoke of a yearning to love and be loved, in all the strength and purity of that much ill-abused word.

She brushed away her tears and brought Barbara a cup of wine, watching her while she drank.

Finally, Barbara stirred herself and asked Maimuna to lead her to the window. They crossed the room and stood staring down at the grounds surrounding the Palace. The huge entrance gates seemed temptingly near, and the branches of a tree reached out and lay only a few feet beneath.

'The tree,' said Maimuna, 'is no more than heartbreak. Look closely.'

Barbara searched the shadows and suddenly saw a movement.

'El Akir leaves the tree to beckon us to escape. He also has a guard beside it.'

Barbara sighed hopelessly and looked at the gates again. The solitary figure of a guard walked across the entrance slowly, his hand on his scimitar, his bearded chin jutting out proudly, illuminated for a brief second or two in the light of a fiery torch, fixed to the outside of the entrance gates.

Ian poised himself in the shadow of some bushes outside the gates, waited until the guard had stepped outside the ring of light then shot out his hands and gripped the man fiercely round the head. Simultaneously, Ibrahim stepped out and drove a delighted fist into the guard's stomach. The guard threshed for a moment, Ian let go and, linking his hands together, brought them down on the back of·the guard's neck. He started to fall and Ibrahim caught him and lowered him quietly to the ground, smiling up at Ian in devilish glee. Ian quickly stripped off the guard's outer clothing and scrambled into it, buckling on the slim belt which held the scimitar and swung the short red cloak behind him and fastened it at the neck. The Arab picked up the guard's pointed helmet and tried it on Ian's head. Finding it to be too big, he snatched at some rags hanging from him, tearing off sufficient to pad the helmet and make it into a passable fit. Ian settled it on his head.

'So far, so good,' he breathed. 'Now, Ibrahim, tie the man up and gag him. Roll him into the bushes so that he's well out of sight. Then steal some horses and bring them as near to the gates as you can, without being seen.'

'Steal some horses, My Lord? Ah, what a partnership you and I would make. I shall steal horses for you.'

Ian turned away and started to adopt the guard's route, walking slowly back and forth in front of the gate. A few minutes later, he saw the shadow of Ibrahim dart away. He had no idea whether he had seen the last of his odd ally or whether he would come up to expectations. He glanced up at a dimly lighted window he could just see through the branches of a tree. He could see the outlines of two women staring down, but it was too dark to see their faces. At least he had a rough idea where the harem was, although he thought it strange it should face out into the grounds. He did not know about El Akir's Tree of Heartbreak. He continued his march, wondering when he could risk leaving his post and make a way into the Palace.

Maimuna said, 'You must be mistaken.'

'No, I'm not, I know I'm not,' Barbara insisted. 'The guard outside the gates had a beard. And now he hasn't one.'

'Perhaps there are two guards.'

Barbara nodded, the moment of interest fading.

Suddenly the double doors of the chamber were thrown open and El Akir walked in. The girls in the room drew

themselves away, standing around the walls of the room, staring with trepidation at the man and the short whip he carried in his right hand.

He moved into the chamber and stopped in the centre of the room, beside a long, low table. He turned and looked at Barbara and Maimuna. A candle wavered and the scar on his face seemed to be blazing out redly.

'Bring her here, Maimuna.'

Barbara pressed the girl gently away, so that she would have no part of what was going to happen, and walked towards the Emir, her heart thudding. There was absolutely no sound in the room except the soft fall of her slippered feet and the slight, insistent tap of the whip on El Akir's leg. She stopped about three feet away from him.

They both stared at each other in the silence that followed. Slowly then, very deliberately, El Akir raised the whip until it was level with his face.

'Your tender flesh,' he said hoarsely, 'is about to feel my first caresses.'

CHAPTER EIGHT

Demons and Sorcerers

The cry just touched Ian's ears. It was half choked back, half mixed with a sob, a sheer expression of pain and anguish – come and gone so quickly he wondered whether he might not have imagined it. He crouched now, just out of reach of the circle of light, straining his ears.

It came again, some violent and dreadful pain forcing more sound out of a tortured body to quell the shocked

activities of heart and brain; a sound that bit its way into the conscience, begging to know why it had been made at all, reaching out a tremulous frond of agony to earn pity and peace, demanding help – yet somehow not pleading for it – for the sound was made in pain and not in fear. Courage and defiance were saturated through the sound.

It was a woman's cry. And just before it, there had been another noise, a slap or a crack of sound, some hard, unyielding matter meeting something else, something softer. Ian's nerves tautened and he felt a thrill of horror playing over them, a ghostly finger touching each tiny strand. In a second he darted through the gates and was lost in the shadows of the grounds outside the main building, quite unaware that as soon as the gate was left unguarded another man appeared and ran through them.

Ian knew he had little chance inside the Palace itself. Whatever rough idea he had about the position of the harem, other guards were sure to be about. One or two he might be able to surprise and bring down, but the chances of being overwhelmed were much too great. He made straight for the tree which grew so conveniently beneath the windows of the harem. A sudden movement alerted him, and he saw the guard straightening up and looking in his direction. As the guard's hand flew down to his scimitar, Ian jumped forward and kicked out fiercely, the point of his boot taking the man in the middle of his solar plexus. The guard jack-knifed with a grunt and Ian fell beyond him, turning desperately to keep his advantage. The guard rolled in torment, struggling to get his breath to call for help. Ian jumped up, drew out his scimitar and brought the hilt of it down on the side of the man's head.

Another moaning cry from above his head spurred him into feverish activity, and he started to clamber up the tree as fast as he could.

The man who had slipped through the gates when Ian had left them had stood watching all this time, puzzled to see one of El Akir's guards behaving so strangely. Then he turned and hurried off, avoiding the Palace itself and making for the stables – for Haroun ed Diin had his own plan carefully worked out.

Ian scrambled upwards, ignoring the twigs and branches that scraped his hands and face, losing his badly-fitting helmet in the desperate rush to reach the top. In the peak of condition, he found his muscles answering every possible demand and some Divine Providence led his hands and feet to safe projections and strong boughs.

The fourth cry was louder now, and not just because he was nearer. He heaved himself upwards and stood on a thick arm of the tree and stared directly into the harem.

He saw a young girl of astounding beauty, tears streaming from her eyes, lying full length on the floor, pulling at the foot of a man who held a whip in his right hand. He saw the man lift his foot slightly and kick the girl away from him, and as his face turned to her, Ian distinctly recognized the livid scar which disfigured his face, knew the man to be El Akir.

Then Ian looked at the girl who was stretched out on her face on a long, low table. The ugly weals showed up across her back and the knuckles of her hands showed white as they gripped the edge of the table, waiting for the next blow to fall. He took in the scene in slow motion, like a film that was being shown at the wrong speed, so great was the shock of the drama in that room.

The girl on the table was Barbara.

Suddenly he heard shouts in the corridor beyond and El Akir cursed and strode to the doors of the chamber. At the same time, Ian heard a gradual roaring somewhere away on his right and a shower of sparks which rocketed into the air told him that a fire had broken out on the other side of the Palace. This was obviously the message being brought to El Akir, for he left the room, slamming the doors behind him with a muttered curse.

Ian immediately seized his opportunity and ran along the arm of the tree and jumped for the window, thankful there was no glass in the way. The girl who had been kicked by El Akir had rushed to Barbara, gesturing to the other girls, who started to hurry across the room. But when Ian appeared, as if by magic, they all stopped.

'Barbara,' he said urgently, jumping down from the window and crossing to her. She opened her eyes, which she'd kept screwed up tight, and stared at Ian as he knelt beside her.

The smile she gave him was a whole book of expressions, the sudden relief in her eyes mingling with an odd look of triumph that he had found her still defiant, still determined, still with plenty of reserves to withstand whatever trials and tortures El Akir could devise.

'Have you something you can put on her back?' said Ian to the girl beside him. She nodded and signalled to the little Indian girl, who ran away to a corner of the room.

'Maimuna, this is Ian,' said Barbara, faintly. 'He's come to take us away.'

Maimuna took hold of one of Ian's hands, raised it to her lips and pressed it against her cheek. The Indian girl hurried to them with a little jar of salve. Maimuna thanked her and took it, asking her to listen closely at the doors and warn them if anyone approached. Then she bent over Barbara's back.

'I will be as soft and gentle as I can,' said Maimuna.

Ian moved around and bent down on one knee, his face near to Barbara's, trying to ignore the little winces she gave as the girl started to smooth on the ointment with quick, deft little gestures.

'Barbara, I'm so sorry. So terribly sorry. But I have horses outside the Palace gates . . . if we can only get to them.'

'Can we climb down the tree?'

'I think it's the best way. If you can manage?'

'Yes.'

She hunched her shoulders sharply, her teeth finding her lower lip, as Maimuna completed the last of her work. Ian unclipped the red cloak from around his throat and spread it over Barbara as she sat up. Ian noticed the sheen of perspiration on her face and he bent and kissed her gently on the forehead.

The little Indian girl suddenly gave an agitated cry and retreated towards them.

'Quickly! You must hide. Someone is coming,' she gasped. The girls in the room all shrank back in their accustomed positions, trying to find what comfort they could from a closeness to the walls; all except Maimuna.

'Take her out of the window,' she said rapidly. 'I will delay him.'

'He'll kill you, Maimuna,' said Barbara.

'My life does not matter.'

'It does matter,' said Ian. 'Stay here with Barbara.'

He drew his scimitar from its scabbard and ran over to the doors, just reaching cover as they were flung open and El Akir marched in arrogantly.

Ian stepped behind him and closed the doors, leaning against them. El Akir slowed to a stop aware that something was amiss. He looked at the red cloak Barbara clutched around herself, knew it as part of the uniform of one of his guards. He felt, rather than saw, that the women in the chamber were gazing at him in some sort of a new way, as if they were waiting for something expectantly.

He swung round, then crouched as he saw Ian. His hand sped down to the sword at his side and he unsheathed it.

'What are you doing in here, carrion?' he spat out viciously. 'Don't you know it's death to be in my harem?'

'Your death!' Ian said.

He took two steps forward and lifted his blade. The Emir parried with a low cut, the two metals scraping together.

'Are you mad?' screamed El Akir, retreating a step or two. Ian made a huge downward cut, his blade flashing

through the air. His opponent cut upwards defensively then twisted his wrist to slash sideways at Ian's legs. Ian jumped up, striking hard at the other's sword hand, just missing, his blade sliding off the hilt with a spark.

'Guards!' roared El Akir. 'To the harem! Guards!' He cut at Ian viciously, who felt the blade skim across his hair as he was forced to duck. He lunged forward, using the scimitar more in the fashion of an *épée* but El Akir knocked it aside and suddenly advanced with a series of hacking cuts and blows that had Ian defending desperately. Their hilts clashed and Ian jumped forward, forcing his weight behind his sword, trying to press both the blades back like scissors around his enemy's neck. El Akir flicked his sword hand expertly and swayed sideways, letting Ian's pressure impel him forwards. Ian staggered off balance and the Emir struck at his back. Ian heard the rip of cloth as the razor edge just grazed his clothes, missing the flesh by a hair's-breadth. It was becoming quite clear that El Akir was a cool, dangerous swordsman, well practised in the art. He now tried to follow up his advantage, but Ian swung round his free hand and clubbed him on the cheek-bone, giving himself a temporary relief as the Emir tottered sideways, shaking his head from the blow.

Ian saw all the girls running now, directed by Maimuna, hurrying to the double doors. Some put their weight against it while others began to drag the couches and the chests and other furniture to block the door.

El Akir realized what they were up to and, thrusting at Ian so that he rocked back on his heels, turned and ran to the doors, his weapon circling above his head, ready to cleave the nearest girl in two. Ian reached down and pulled desperately at the rug and his enemy staggered and fell on one knee, giving Ian time to interpose himself and defend the girls. A hammer of blows descended on the other side of the door and a gruff voice shouted the Emir's name.

'Break down the door, you fools,' he yelled, cutting once

again at Ian, who eluded the attack with nimble footwork and responded so hard that he drew blood from a slight cut he made on El Akir's left shoulder. The Emir smashed at Ian's right leg, fortunately with the flat side of his scimitar but nevertheless numbing it. Seeing that Ian was handicapped for a moment, El Akir suddenly darted to one side and seized hold of Maimuna by the hair and pulled her off her feet. Ian made a desperate attempt to sever his enemy's head from his body, but the blade swung away a foot short and El Akir dragged the screaming girl to the window. He pulled her, half fainting, to her feet, letting go of her hair and gripping her round the throat with his free arm.

The pounding on the doors was stronger now as more bodies were hurled against it. El Akir shouted to them to double their efforts then pointed his scimitar at Ian who was steadily approaching.

'One more step and I'll cut this girl in two.'

Ian looked at Barbara anxiously. She had managed to sit upright properly now, although unable to move without a hundred pokers of pain stabbing through her. Ian saw a change in her eyes, a slight frown and then realization as she raised her eyebrows. He looked quickly at El Akir for the answer. Behind him began to emerge the shape of a large, poorly dressed man, entering the harem by the same route Ian had taken.

Haroun stood on the window and put his hands round El Akir's throat, so surprising him that the sword dropped out of his hand in terror. The man exerted all his strength and lifted the Emir off his feet.

For a second the two men were poised, El Akir pulling feebly at the hands around his throat, his tongue forced out between his teeth, his scar glaring redly as the blood pounded in his head. Then Haroun jumped down from the window, at the same time twisting his hands to the right. As his feet touched the ground, he pivoted, whirling El Akir like a throwing hammer. Suddenly he let go and fell on one knee.

El Akir hurtled through the air with a ghastly scream of fear and smashed high up into the wall opposite. There was a sickening thud as the Emir's head struck the wall, then the body rebounded and slammed to the ground.

Haroun clasped his daughter in his arms and beckoned to Ian impatiently. Ian took hold of Barbara's hand and hurried her to the window.

Despite the high pile of furniture the double doors were beginning to move slightly now, the men outside battering it in with something heavy.

The girls began to retreat, looking at Ian for guidance. Ian waved them to the window and grinned at Haroun.

'I don't know who you are,' said Ian, 'but you've made a friend. The girls can help each other down, while we give them as much of a chance as possible.'

Haroun nodded, an answering smile on his face. He urged Barbara, Maimuna and the girls to make their way down the tree and out of the gates, as fast as they could.

'The guards who aren't in the passage are busy fighting the fire I started in the hay-barn,' he stated as the last girl disappeared.

Ian threw down his sword and ran over and collected up three of the small oil-lamps nearest to him. Their flames fluttered as he hurried to the double doors, splintering now as the men outside put all their strength into breaking through. Haroun saw what Ian was doing and fetched some more lamps and together they threw them at the pile of furniture. The lamps spilled out their oil and ignited, and soon a blaze was roaring. Ian ran back and picked up his sword, sheathed it and gestured to Haroun to precede him out of the window. Haroun replied with a push.

'You go first, or I'll throw you out,' he growled.

'I'd rather climb, thanks,' grinned Ian and scrambled out and on to the bough. Beneath him, he could just see the running shapes of the harem girls, rushing towards the gates.

He and Haroun clambered down the tree and followed them.

As soon as they were outside, Ibrahim appeared and urged Ian to help him swing the great doors to a close. Then the Arab produced a thick bar of wood and he wedged it between the outer handles.

'You see, I am here, My Lord, just as I promised,' he beamed. Ian put a hand on his shoulder and smiled at him. Then Haroun hurried to them.

'Don't stand here dreaming!' He turned to the Arab. 'The soldiers will be all around us, you half-wit!'

'This half-wit has stolen all their horses, master.'

'They can still use their legs then.'

'But they cannot come through these doors. This half-wit has seen to that as well.'

'And is there no other way out of the Palace?'

The Arab looked suitably disturbed.

'This half-wit hadn't thought of that!'

He led them quickly to where he had tethered the horses, some twenty in number and more than they'd need. They heard the sound of a mass of running feet.

'The rest of the guard,' gasped the Arab. 'They are returning from the Old Quarter.'

The three men helped all the girls to mount and with Ibrahim leading and Ian and Haroun bringing up the rear the party of seven girls and three men made their way out of Lydda.

A half-hour's ride without pursuit of any kind and Haroun took over the lead, directing the party to where he had left Safiya in a little orange orchard. Maimuna and her sister fell into each other's arms tenderly. Ian decided they could risk a five-minute rest, but no longer he warned Haroun.

'Probably we are out of danger,' observed Haroun, 'although you are wise to be cautious. It is my opinion that the guards will be quarrelling amongst themselves now the El Akir is dead.'

The party rode onward, making a longer journey of three hours this time. The night was clear with a strong moon and the stars were strung out like fairy lights. There was absolutely no movement in the air, not even a puff of wind, but the temperature had dropped and all the girls were half frozen in the flimsy costumes they wore.

The route Haroun took was a circuitous one, deliberately taking the longest and the most difficult paths to confuse any possible pursuers. Once he led them down a stream for fully a mile, twisting and turning with the course of it, keeping the party firmly in the water so that no tell-tale hoof-marks were left on either of the shallow muddy banks. Finally, where the stream began to broaden out, obviously becoming a tributary, he ordered them to guide their horses over a patch of shingle and towards a cleft in some rocks overlooking the water.

Satisfied now that everything had been done to disguise their escape, he set them all galloping forward. There was no talk for each one was concentrating on resisting the cold in his or her own way, quite apart from the eye-straining business of the constant searching of the ground ahead. Some of the girls bore the journey better than others, the Negress best of all, sitting hunched over her animal, her head bent steadily on the ground just ahead of her and following directly behind Haroun, echoing his warnings to be careful of this loose rock or that sudden depression in the ground. Maimuna and Safiya rode just ahead of Ibrahim, the elder girl's left hand firmly clasped in her sister's right, occasionally turning their heads towards each other as if to reassure themselves they were together again.

The worst to suffer was Barbara. Although the cloak Ian had thrown around her kept out the cold well enough, it rubbed against the wounds on her back. The movement of her body itself was bad enough, but the two together were an almost unbearable agony.

Finally, Haroun called the party to a halt and dismounted

at the edge of a wood, telling them all to wait for him. They huddled together, making a ring of the horses, keeping themselves as warm as they could.

Haroun reappeared after a few minutes and led them all through the trees, Ibrahim bringing up the rear with the horses. Eventually, they came to a ramshackle old wooden building.

'It looks far worse than it is,' he announced, 'but the walls and the roof are good enough to keep out the cold, and we shall soon have a fire blazing.'

Ian led Barbara in and cleared away a space in one corner which was covered in dead leaves and some musty old hay. Ibrahim appeared with the horses' blankets and together they made a bed for Barbara to lie face down on. She collapsed on to it with a shuddering sigh of relief and fell into an immediate sleep.

Haroun, who had been out foraging in the wood, returned with an armful of dead branches and twigs and started a fire.

'I used to use this place, with other caravan leaders, sometimes,' he told Ian, as he fed some bigger pieces of wood into the flames. Safiya appeared beside him, undoing a saddlebag filled with dried meat and fruit and she started to apportion it out as carefully and as fairly as she could.

'I see you came well prepared,' said Ian with a smile.

'Either I meant to bring back my daughter and your friend Barbara – or die!' Haroun answered briefly. 'Fortunately I allowed provision for a long journey, thinking we would need to travel for many days if we were pursued.'

'There will still only be just enough to go round, Father,' said Safiya. She began to distribute the food, a piece of meat, some bread and some dates for each person, and soon they were all eating hungrily, except Barbara, who slept deeply now, and peacefully.

Haroun moved over to Maimuna and sat himself on the rough floor. The other girls were settling down as comfortably as they could and gradually one after another fell asleep. Ibrahim lay against one of the walls, his head dropping over his chest, resting his forehead on his bent knees, snoring slightly. Ian lay by the door, the scimitar close to his hand, determined not to leave anything to chance now that they had achieved so much.

Maimuna stared at her father, tears rushing to her eyes; then he put his arm around her, soothing away her sobbing until her head cradled on his massive chest and she, too, fell asleep. Haroun laid her down to the ground, gently, so as not to wake her, and moved over to Ian at the door, settling himself so that they could talk together quietly without disturbing the others.

'A motley collection, Ian, my friend,' he said, gazing about the room.

'What can be done for the girls from the harem?'

'Fortunately, I am a rich man. My wealth lies with friends in Damascus, held for me until I made my settlement with El Akir. Oh, I shall not set up a harem of my own,' he went on, giving Ian a sudden smile. 'I shall become their patron and either see them married well or return them to their own homes and families.'

'I have one favour to ask you,' said Ian. He pointed across at Ibrahim. Haroun nodded.

'I know the man. He is a disgraceful thief and a scoundrel but I will see he is well rewarded for helping us. I cannot tempt you into coming to Damascus, you and your lady Barbara? I have a thriving business of which you could become a part.' He looked down at his hands, 'There would be no son to rival you.'

There was a pause, for Ian felt he couldn't turn down the man's generous offer too rapidly. He let the silence pretend he was considering the matter.

'I can't see how we could do that,' he said at last, 'much as we'd want to. I have two other friends to look after. Your search is over, Haroun, but mine still has some way to go.'

'What will you do?'

'Give Barbara all the rest she needs and then ride for Jaffa. There's a little wood outside the town we shall visit first, in case my friends are there waiting for us.'

In the morning, Barbara found her sleep had completely refreshed her, and the salve Maimuna had spread on her back had done so much to ease the pain she found she could move quite well, suffering no more than a dull ache.

The parting was a sad one, Maimuna and Safiya begging them to change their minds. Surprisingly, Ibrahim was genuinely distressed at having to say good-bye to Ian, and not even the promise of a handsome reward from Haroun seemed to console him. The harem girls had come to regard Ian as the symbol of their release, a lucky charm without which they would all fall into evil hands again. But finally the tears and kisses came to an end and Haroun led them all away, deep into the heart of the forest, while Ian and Barbara sat on their horses watching until the last glimpse faded and the trees swallowed them up. The calls of good-bye and the accompanying clop of the horses' hooves became fainter and fainter and were gradually replaced by the silence of the forest.

Barbara looked across at Ian, stretched out a hand and held his. A dozen unsaid words hung between them in the understanding of that moment. Modern people though they were, they had stepped into a world of chivalry and barbarism and Ian had not failed her. She had needed him and he had come for her. She knew, whatever the age, whatever the place, whatever the circumstances, he would measure up to her every expectation.

She leant across from her horse, put her arm around his neck and kissed him softly on the lips. She sat back again, her heart beating a little faster, a slight tinge of pink at her cheeks, holding his eyes with hers.

Then they rode towards Jaffa.

* * * * *

The Doctor lay quietly beneath the tangle of broken branches, his hand just touching Vicki's. Ahead of him, about twenty yards away, a soldier was leaning against a tree, polishing his sword with a rough cloth.

The voices of other men intruded on the peace of the little wood, the rattle of armaments and the occasional snort of a horse – sounds indicating the presence of a body of men. Beyond the solitary soldier who was working so industriously was the tall ring of bushes hiding the *Tardis*. Twenty yards from safety. It was worse than twenty miles, thought the Doctor gloomily.

He and Vicki had had such good luck, too, in their flight from Jaffa. They had dodged and manœuvred through the town, just keeping out of reach of the Earl of Leicester's men. And then the Doctor had remembered the shopkeeper, Ben Daheer. Slipping through the patrols, he had guided Vicki to the shop, told its owner that he and his ward wished to travel incognito and persuaded Ben Daheer to give them complete changes of clothes and some provisions for the journey. Receiving their expensive clothes in exchange for some clean but very well-worn monks' habits and a little food made a good bargain and he even went so far as to show them a private route out of Jaffa, wishing them every success on their 'pilgrimage', for the Doctor had pretended that he had a burning desire to visit Mecca.

They made the journey to the little wood in good time, their spirits soaring, convinced they had eluded their enemies. Just as they reached the cover of the trees, a body of horsemen had galloped into sight with the Earl of Leicester at its head, and before the Doctor and Vicki could run to where the *Tardis* was hidden, the Earl's men had set themselves down right in front of it, effectively barring them from reaching it.

They made no attempt to search the wood, although the Doctor knew that would be their next step. He assured

Vicki that they didn't know about the existence of the ship. He had already worked out what had happened. Leicester, convinced that the Doctor was an agent working for Saladin, had collected all the information he knew about the Doctor as soon as it was clear that he had slipped through his fingers. The only clue he had was that the Doctor had first made himself known in the wood, and seizing upon that as a last hope had ridden there with some men. The Doctor confirmed his assumption by stealthily climbing a tree and eavesdropping on the Earl talking to some of his soldiers.

'These two are spies undoubtedly; sent by Saladin to learn our secrets,' he told them. 'If I have judged correctly they will come this way again.'

'They will not pass by,' growled one of the soldiers, and the Earl nodded approvingly.

'Well said! For they have had opportunity to study the numbers of our army in Jaffa and make details of our stores and equipment, all vitally important to the Saracens. Spread yourselves about and let your ears be sharp and alert.'

The Doctor had retired, raging inwardly, and he and Vicki had then found the safest spot they could and covered themselves with leaves and broken branches, lying as near the ship as possible in the hope that they might be able to evade Leicester's men and slam the doors of the *Tardis* in their faces. Then all they would have to do would be to wait for Ian and Barbara to arrive (for both of them were quite convinced they would, in time) and worry about admitting them when the occasion demanded.

The strong aroma of roasting meat began to drift through the trees, and the soldier put away his sword, reminded of his hunger. He moved forward uncertainly, then strolled in the direction of the cooking. The Doctor's fingers tapped on the girl's hand. She crept out from beneath the branches carefully, spread the bushes aside and looked about her. The

Doctor whispered to her and she raced across the opening and disappeared through the ring of bushes.

The Doctor nodded to himself and eased his cramped legs slightly. It seemed he had lain like this for hours, enduring the bitter cold of the night, dozing fitfully in the early morning sun. Now the heat of the afternoon poured down, bringing out beads of perspiration on his forehead, and his heavy monk's habit felt damp and sticky. He crawled out from the camouflage of twigs and leaves and peered about – everything seemed quiet and deserted. He bunched up the front of his robe and started to run across the little clearing. At that moment the soldier wandered into view and with a shout of triumph charged forward and grabbed hold of the Doctor by the scruff of his neck. In a second the clearing was full of soldiers.

The Doctor never panicked in emergencies and stood quietly now, facing his enemies. The Earl of Leicester pushed his way through the ring of grinning soldiers, a look of triumph on his face.

'I thought you would show yourself, traitor!'

'I'm no traitor,' said the Doctor calmly. 'What do you want with me?'

Leicester scowled at him and put his hands on his hips.

'First, I want the truth and then I shall rid this world of you.'

'I will tell you the truth about this man,' said a quiet voice. Leicester swung around.

Ian walked towards the group. Just visible behind him were two horses, and the Doctor could see Barbara slowly dismounting.

'I am Sir Ian, Knight of Jaffa, charged by King Richard to intercede with Saladin on behalf of Sir William des Preaux and a lady who had fallen into Saracen hands.'

'I remember you,' said Leicester, 'for I conducted you to the King on your arrival with a wounded knight. But as I recall the events you were this man's companion.'

'That is not true,' said Ian. 'We met in this wood and he helped me carry the injured knight, de Tornebu, to Jaffa. But his smiles and willing hands were only a disguise to ingratiate himself. He desired nothing more than to worm his way into the confidence of the King.'

'I thought so,' roared Leicester, his face black with fury.

'I have discovered he is worse than a spy,' remarked Ian, moving nearer to the Doctor. Every eye was on Ian now, but the Doctor just caught a glimpse of Barbara stepping through the ring of bushes and disappearing out of sight.

'He is a sorcerer,' said Ian, dropping his voice.

There was a silence. One or two of the soldiers moved back slightly in superstitious awe, while Leicester's hand fell on the hilt of his sword.

'Then let us dispatch him and have done with it.'

'My Lord of Leicester, I have travelled a long way with but one ambition.'

'To watch this man's execution?'

'No, My Lord. To administer it.'

The Doctor stood silently, making absolutely no contribution to the conversation, his eyes staring steadily into Ian's.

'You would deprive me of a pleasure, Sir Ian,' said Leicester doggedly.

'But it was he who arranged the ambush on King Richard in this very wood,' replied Ian. 'It was he who was responsible for the lady, Barbara, being abducted. The greater debt is to me, My Lord, and it can only be met with his life and my sword.'

Leicester nodded. 'This villainy knows no bounds. Do it, then, Sir Ian and we will ride back to the King and relate this story.'

Ian moved up to the Doctor. 'Where will you meet your end?'

The Doctor shrugged.

'Let it be a matter between the two of us,' he replied quietly. 'Behind those bushes.'

Ian nodded and drew his sword. He followed the Doctor to the ring of bushes and followed him through them.

As soon as the foliage covered them, the Doctor picked up his robe and ran for the *Tardis*, where Barbara and Vicki were waiting.

The Doctor produced the ship's key from a cord round his neck, opened the doors and they hurried inside, Vicki's excited breath of laughter echoing out as the doors closed behind them.

On the other side of the bushes the Earl of Leicester stiffened.

'Did any of you hear another voice?' he demanded. 'A voice . . . that laughed?'

The men looked at each other nervously. Leicester drew out his sword and forced his way through the bushes, his men crowding in behind him. They stopped in alarm as they stared at the extraordinary spectacle of the telephone box. A light began to flash on the top of it, and with one accord they fell to their knees.

Then the box faded and disappeared in front of their eyes and in a second there was no evidence that it had been there at all.

'Witchcraft!' muttered Leicester hoarsely. 'Poor Sir Ian! Brave fellow. Spirited away by fiends and black arts.'

He stood up then looked commandingly at the trembling men around him.

'We will not speak of this. Let this story die here in this wood or we'll be branded idiots – or liars.'

The men scrambled to their feet and crashed through the bushes, intent on putting as much space as they could between themselves and the accursed place. Leicester stood silently for a moment, clutching his sword just beneath its hilt and holding it straight out in front of him.

'Poor Sir Ian,' he repeated. 'What dreadful anguish and despair you must be suffering now.'

At that very moment, Ian and the Doctor were trying to

quell the bubbles of laughter that threatened to burst their blood vessels. The Doctor puffed and panted out his pleasure at the way Ian had used his wits and fooled Leicester, while Ian held his side and endeavoured to control himself. The two girls sat side by side on the couch smiling happily.

Finally, the two men recovered, knowing it was more the extent of their relief than any genuine humour at the situation which caused the outburst. They sat around as they were; the Doctor and Vicki in their monks' habits, Ian in his motley costume, half Saracen guard, half English knight, Barbara with the red cloak wrapped around her, the flimsy transparent coverings on her arms and legs bearing the travel stains of her escape from Lydda. They related their adventures to each other, matching this action with that happening, describing one character, revelling in another; passing from incident to incident and adventure to adventure until the stories met and ended with their last fortunate meeting in the wood.

Then Ian and Barbara went off to their rooms to bathe and change, leaving the Doctor to fuss around his controls. Vicki sat on the couch for a while, silent with her thoughts.

'Richard the Lionheart never recaptured Jerusalem, did he, Doctor?' she said eventually.

'No, but he came very near to it, my child,' he replied, his fingers brushing gently over his beloved switches and levers, conscious of the healthy hum of the controls, sure that his Time and Space machine was responding accurately to every impulse.

Finally he turned and leaned against the control column, smiling at Vicki. He thought of his granddaughter, Susan, for a moment, who had sat in that exact position so many times before.

'He faced the Holy City, and then shielded his eyes,' he said.

'Yes, I remember reading that somewhere. But why? He

had come so far . . . why didn't he do what he'd set out to do?'

'Frankly, I think Richard knew he could conquer the city but couldn't hold it. I believe he estimated what the capture of Jerusalem would do – arouse a shout of praise and hope throughout the Christian world. But against this he had to put the dreadful shock it would be to his world's morale when Saladin recaptured it again. People always remember the last battle, my child. No, Richard was right to do what he did.'

Vicki stood up and moved nearer the Doctor, staring fascinated at the lights that flashed and the wheels that spun, a constant source of never-ending delight to her.

'And where do we go now, Doctor?'

He smiled and shook his head, the only answer he would give.

And the *Tardis* flashed on its way, hurtling through the galaxies of Space, spinning through the barriers of Time, searching for a new resting-place on a fresh horizon.

STAY
ON

Here are details of other exciting TARGET titles. If you cannot obtain these books from your local bookshop, or newsagent, write to the address below listing the titles you would like and enclosing cheque or postal order— *not* currency—including 5p per book to cover postage and packing. Postage is free for orders in excess of three titles.

TARGET BOOKS,
Universal-Tandem Publishing Co.,
14 Gloucester Road,
London SW7 4RD

DOCTOR WHO   25p
David Whitaker

(based on the famous BBC television series)

0 426 10110 3   **A Target Adventure**

DOCTOR WHO's first exciting adventure with the Daleks! Ian Chesterton and Barbara Wright travel with the mysterious DOCTOR WHO, and his grand-daughter Susan, to the planet of Skaro in the space-time machine, *Tardis*. There they strive to save the peace-loving Thals from the evil intentions of the hideous Daleks. Can they succeed? And what is more important, will they ever again see their native Earth? *Illustrated.*

If you enjoyed this book and would like to have information sent you about other TARGET titles, write to the address below.

You will also receive:

A FREE TARGET BADGE!

Based on the TARGET BOOKS symbol—see front cover of this book—this attractive three-colour badge, pinned to your blazer-lapel, or jumper, will excite the interest and comment of all your friends!

and you will be further entitled to:

FREE ENTRY INTO THE TARGET DRAW!

All you have to do is cut off the coupon beneath, write on it your name and address *in block capitals*, and pin it to your letter. You will be advised of your lucky draw number. Twice a year, in June and December, numbers will be drawn 'from the hat' and the winner will receive a complete year's set of TARGET books.

Write to: TARGET BOOKS,
        Universal-Tandem Publishing Co.,
        14 Gloucester Road,
        London SW7 4RD

———————————— cut here ————————————

Full name...

Address...

....

...............................County...............................

Age.................................